CW01431689

Table of Contents

Table of Contents

1 Chapter 1: The Sunken City

Sunlight, fractured and diffused by the fathoms of ocean above, painted an ethereal, wavering landscape across the ruins of Syren Reef. Coral, in hues unknown to the surface world, clung to the crumbling marble structures, pulsating with a life that defied the city's watery grave. Schools of iridescent fish darted through broken archways and empty window frames, their scales catching the muted light like scattered jewels. This was no ordinary reef; this was a city, a civilization swallowed by the sea, yet stubbornly refusing to relinquish its grandeur. For centuries it lay undisturbed, a forgotten legend whispered by sailors in hushed tones.

An expedition, funded by the eccentric historian Professor Armitage, had finally located the reef, guided by ancient charts and the persistent local tales. He believed, with a fervor bordering on obsession, that Syren Reef was the key to unlocking the mystery of Atlantis. His theories, initially dismissed by the academic community, now held a tangible weight as the expedition's submersible descended through the crystal-clear waters, revealing the undeniable evidence of a lost civilization. Armitage, his face pressed against the submersible's viewing port, felt a thrill course through him. He was witnessing history unfold.

The submersible touched down on a wide, paved plaza, now carpeted in a thick layer of bioluminescent algae. Strange symbols, unlike any known language, were etched into the remaining pillars and walls. As the expedition team ventured out, their specialized diving suits allowing them to move freely, a sense of awe settled over them. This wasn't merely a collection of ruins, it was a city frozen in time, a ghostly testament to a vanished people. They explored crumbling temples, their once-vibrant frescoes now softened by the ceaseless caress of the ocean currents. They marveled at the intricate mosaics adorning the floors of grand halls, depicting scenes of a sophisticated and powerful society. Every discovery fueled their curiosity, deepening the mystery of Atlantis.

Within the heart of the city, they found a vast, circular chamber. A single, enormous pearl rested upon a pedestal in the center, radiating a soft, otherworldly glow. As they approached, the pearl seemed to pulse with an inner light, and a low hum filled the chamber, resonating deep within their chests. This was the source of the whispers, they realized, the whispers of Triton, god of the sea. The whispers, faint at first, grew in intensity, weaving themselves into a coherent narrative – a prophecy. The prophecy spoke of a golden age, a time of unparalleled prosperity and peace for Atlantis, a time yet to come. But it also warned of dangers, of trials and tribulations that must be overcome before this golden age could be realized. The prophecy spoke of a powerful artifact, the Golden Trident of Poseidon, lost somewhere within the city's ruins. It was the key, the whispers insisted, to unlocking Atlantis's true potential and ushering in the golden age.

The expedition team, invigorated by this revelation, began a meticulous search of the city. Days turned into weeks, and the initial excitement gradually gave way to a weary determination. The city was vast, its secrets well-guarded by the sea. They deciphered more of the strange symbols, learning fragments of Atlantean history and culture. They discovered ingenious engineering feats, advanced technologies lost to time. They found evidence of a people who lived in harmony with the ocean, harnessing its power while respecting its might. With every discovery, their respect for this lost civilization deepened, and their determination to fulfill the prophecy grew stronger.

Finally, in a hidden chamber beneath the royal palace, they found it. The Golden Trident, radiating a warm, golden light, rested on an altar of polished coral. Its three prongs, crafted from an unknown metal that shimmered with an inner fire, reached towards the ceiling, as if yearning to pierce the ocean's surface and reclaim its place in the world above. As Professor Armitage reached out to take the Trident, a tremor shook the city. The ground beneath their feet buckled, sending clouds of silt swirling through the water. From the shadows, a monstrous figure emerged, its eyes glowing with malevolent intent. The whispers grew urgent, warning of the guardian of the Trident, a creature spawned from the depths of the ocean, bound to protect the artifact from unworthy hands. The adventurers knew, with a chilling certainty, that their journey had just begun. They had found the key to Atlantis's golden age, but claiming it would require courage, cunning, and perhaps, a touch of divine intervention. The adventure had only begun. The whispers of Triton, now echoing in their minds, promised both glory and peril in the chapters to come.

1.1   Discovery of Syren Reef

Sunlight, fractured and shimmering, danced on the ocean's surface. The research vessel, The Argo, bobbed gently, a solitary speck amidst the vast expanse of the Aegean Sea. Dr. Aris Thorne, a man whose weathered face spoke of years spent battling the elements, peered intently at the sonar readings. An anomaly, a cluster of unusual formations unlike anything he'd encountered, pulsed on the screen. He leaned closer, adjusting his glasses, a thrill of anticipation electrifying the air. Could this be it? Could this be the legendary Syren Reef, the gateway to the lost city of Atlantis?

For decades, Thorne had dedicated his life to this pursuit, pouring over ancient texts, nautical charts, and whispered legends. He had faced ridicule from his peers, accusations of chasing phantoms, but his conviction remained unshaken. The whispers of Atlantis, a city of unimaginable beauty and advanced technology swallowed by the sea, had captivated him since childhood. Now, the sonar pulsed with increasing intensity, painting a vivid picture of a complex reef system, far too intricate to be a natural formation. It was a symphony of coral arches, spiraling towers, and vast, open plazas, all hinting at a forgotten civilization.

He called to his first mate, a young, enthusiastic oceanographer named Eleni Dimitriou. Her expertise in marine geology had been invaluable to the expedition. "Eleni, come take a look at this," he said, his voice barely containing his excitement. Eleni rushed to his side, her eyes widening as she studied the readings. A shared look of wonder passed between them. This was more than just a reef; it was an underwater city, waiting to be rediscovered. The implications were staggering.

With a sense of shared purpose, they initiated the dive sequence. The submersible, Triton, was prepped and lowered into the crystalline waters. Inside, Thorne and Eleni descended into the depths, the world outside their viewport transitioning from brilliant turquoise to a deep, ethereal blue. As they approached the reef, the sonar readings transformed into breathtaking reality. Gigantic coral structures, pulsating with bioluminescent life, rose before them like the skeletal remains of ancient skyscrapers. Schools of vibrant fish darted through arched doorways and windows, adding splashes of color to the otherwise muted palette of the deep. It was a scene of haunting beauty, a testament to a civilization lost to time.

They navigated Triton through a colossal archway, its surface covered in intricate carvings that seemed to shift and writhe in the submersible's lights. The arch opened into a vast plaza, paved with what appeared to be polished marble, now covered in a thin layer of sediment. Statues, eroded but still majestic, lined the perimeter, their faces frozen in expressions of serene contemplation. One statue, significantly larger than the others, depicted a figure holding a trident, its features strikingly similar to the depictions of Poseidon Thorne had seen in ancient Greek art.

Eleni maneuvered the submersible closer to one of the smaller statues, its hand outstretched as if offering a welcome. A shiver ran down Thorne's spine. He felt an inexplicable connection to this place, a sense of coming home. He extended the submersible's robotic arm and gently brushed away the sediment from the statue's hand, revealing an inscription written in a language he didn't recognize. He photographed the inscription, knowing it would be crucial to deciphering the mysteries of this lost city.

As they continued their exploration, they discovered more evidence of a sophisticated civilization. Intricate canals crisscrossed the city, suggesting a complex system of water management. Buildings of varying sizes and shapes hinted at different social strata and purposes. One structure, resembling a massive amphitheater, stood at the heart of the plaza, its tiers carved into the living coral. It was a city built in harmony with the ocean, a testament to the ingenuity and artistry of its inhabitants.

They collected samples of the coral, the sediment, and anything else that might shed light on the city's history. Hours passed in a blur of discovery and awe. As the sun began to set, casting long shadows across the ocean floor, they reluctantly began their ascent. The Syren Reef, once a whisper in the annals of history, was now a tangible reality, a city resurrected from the depths. The discovery was just the beginning. The secrets of Atlantis, Thorne knew, were waiting to be unveiled. Back on board The Argo, Thorne and Eleni shared their findings with the rest of the crew. Excitement rippled through the vessel. They had found Syren Reef, the gateway to Atlantis. The journey had just begun.

1.2   The Whispers of Triton

The rhythmic susurrus began subtly, a faint murmur beneath the currents, a tremor in the deep. It danced along Alexi's skin, a caress of sound that tugged at his awareness, drawing him from the study of the ancient, barnacle-encrusted map spread before him. The whispers, barely audible at first, grew in intensity, weaving themselves into coherent words, a language older than any he knew yet somehow intrinsically understood. They spoke of Triton, son of Poseidon, herald of the deep, and his urgent message for the seekers of the lost city. Triton's voice resonated with the power of the ocean itself, carrying an echo of ancient magic and the weight of forgotten ages. This was no ordinary sound; it was a summons, a call to destiny.

Alexi, a scholar of forgotten lore and cryptic texts, recognized the unique signature of Atlantean magic in the whispers. He had dedicated his life to uncovering the truth behind the myths, driven by an insatiable curiosity and a yearning to connect with a past shrouded in mystery. The discovery of Syren Reef, a geological anomaly that defied explanation, had ignited a spark of hope within him, a belief that the legends of Atlantis were more than just stories. Now, with Triton's whispers echoing in his mind, he felt an unshakeable certainty that he was on the verge of a monumental discovery. The whispers guided him, painting a vivid image of a hidden passage beneath the reef, a gateway to the sunken city. They spoke of trials and tribulations that awaited him, dangers lurking in the shadows, and guardians protecting the city's secrets. Yet, despite the warnings, a sense of profound peace settled over Alexi. He understood that this journey was not just about finding Atlantis; it was about rediscovering a lost part of himself, a connection to a heritage he never knew he possessed. The whispers promised knowledge and power, a chance to unlock the mysteries of a civilization lost to time.

He glanced at his companions, Isabella, a seasoned marine archaeologist, and Kaelen, a master diver and navigator. Their faces reflected the same awe and determination that mirrored his own. They too heard Triton's call, their individual skills and knowledge converging at this pivotal moment. Isabella meticulously charted the coordinates provided by the whispers, her fingers tracing the contours of the reef with practiced ease. Kaelen prepared the submersible, ensuring every system was in optimal condition, his movements precise and efficient. They were a team bound by a shared purpose, ready to face whatever challenges lay ahead.

The submersible descended into the inky depths, leaving behind the shimmering surface world for the cold embrace of the ocean's abyss. The whispers grew stronger, guiding them through a labyrinth of underwater canyons and caverns, revealing a path invisible to ordinary eyes. The pressure mounted, the darkness deepened, yet their resolve remained unshaken. They were driven by the promise of discovery, by the echoes of a glorious past waiting to be unearthed. As they approached the reef, a faint luminescence emanated from its depths, illuminating a hidden passage, an entrance to a world forgotten by time. Triton's whispers had led them to the gateway of Atlantis, a city shimmering with ethereal light, a testament to the enduring power of myth and legend. It was a sight that would forever be etched in their memories, a beacon of hope in the vast, mysterious ocean. The whispers, now softer, promised more secrets to unfold, more wonders to behold, as they ventured deeper into the heart of the sunken city. This was just the beginning of their extraordinary journey, a prelude to the grand adventure that awaited them within the realm of Atlantis. They were ready to embrace the unknown, to unravel the mysteries of a lost civilization, and to reclaim the legacy that was rightfully theirs. The golden age of Atlantis was within their grasp, waiting to be resurrected from the depths of time.

1.3   A Prophecy Unveiled

The air crackled with an almost tangible energy. Salt spray misted across the ancient stones of Syren Reef, clinging to the weathered carvings that hinted at a civilization lost to time. We huddled closer, the group of us a motley collection of historians, archaeologists, and treasure hunters, united by the lure of the unknown. Professor Armitage, his face illuminated by the flickering lantern, traced a finger across a glyph etched deep into a submerged pillar. This, he declared, his voice hushed with awe, was the key.

The glyph, a stylized wave cresting over a sun, resonated with the whispers we had heard since arriving at Syren Reef. Stories of a sunken city, a golden age lost, and a prophecy that spoke of its return. These whispers, carried on the ocean breeze and murmured by the tides, had drawn us here, each of us driven by our own motivations – fortune, glory, or simply the thirst for knowledge. Now, standing on the precipice of discovery, the whispers felt less like myth and more like a tangible reality, pulsating with the promise of something extraordinary.

Professor Armitage, his lifelong obsession with Atlantis finally within reach, began to decipher the inscription. The ancient Atlantean language, he explained, was remarkably similar to ancient Greek, but with a unique melodic structure, almost as if designed to be sung rather than spoken. He translated the inscription phrase by phrase, his voice rising with excitement as the meaning became clear. It spoke of a time of unparalleled prosperity, a reign of peace and wisdom, an era when Atlantis stood as a beacon of enlightenment for the entire world. This, the inscription proclaimed, was the Golden Age.

But the inscription went further, detailing not only the past glory of Atlantis, but its future resurgence. It spoke of a chosen one, a hero who would rise from the depths of despair to reclaim the lost legacy and usher in a new Golden Age. This hero, the inscription foretold, would wield a powerful artifact, the Golden Trident of Poseidon, and would vanquish a formidable foe, the war god Ares, who had plunged Atlantis into darkness. The prophecy was intricate, woven with symbolic language and cryptic allusions, yet its core message resonated with a clarity that sent shivers down our spines.

The prophecy also spoke of trials and tribulations, of dangers that lay hidden beneath the waves. It warned of treacherous creatures, cunning sorcerers, and the seductive allure of forgotten magic. These challenges, the inscription implied, would test the chosen one's strength, courage, and wisdom, forging him into the leader Atlantis needed. The weight of this responsibility, even for a hero yet to be revealed, felt palpable in the heavy air. We exchanged glances, each of us pondering the implications of this ancient prophecy. Was it mere legend, a fantastical tale passed down through generations? Or was it a roadmap to a future yet to be written? The discovery of Syren Reef and the unveiling of this prophecy had opened a Pandora's Box of possibilities, a blend of hope and trepidation that settled upon us like the mist clinging to the ancient stones.

The final lines of the inscription described the signs that would herald the return of the Golden Age: the awakening of ancient sea creatures, the alignment of celestial bodies, and the rediscovery of Syren Reef itself. As Professor Armitage finished the translation, a vibrant double rainbow arced across the sky, its colors reflecting in the calm waters surrounding the reef. We stared in stunned silence, the vibrant display mirroring the hope that blossomed within us. The prophecy was not just a story; it was a call to action, a beacon illuminating the path toward a future we could scarcely imagine. The Golden Age of Atlantis was not just a legend; it was a destiny waiting to be fulfilled. The inscription on the stone, bathed in the ethereal light of the rainbow, seemed to pulse with a newfound energy, beckoning us forward into the unknown. The whispers of Triton, once faint and elusive, now resonated with a powerful urgency, guiding us toward a future intertwined with the fate of a lost civilization. The journey ahead promised to be perilous, yet the potential rewards, the restoration of a legendary Golden Age, were too significant to ignore. We stood on the threshold of a grand adventure, our hearts pounding with anticipation, ready to face the challenges that lay ahead and embrace the destiny that awaited us in the depths of the forgotten city.

2 Chapter 2: The Serpent's Curse

Sunlight, fractured by the churning waters above, dappled the cavern floor in an eerie, shifting mosaic. Corals, twisted into grotesque shapes resembling writhing snakes, pulsed with an unnatural luminescence. This was Medusa's Lair, a place whispered about in hushed tones by even the bravest of Atlantean mariners. A place of perverse beauty, where life and death danced a macabre tango. We moved cautiously, our small band clinging to the rocky path that snaked through the heart of the cavern. The air hung heavy, thick with the scent of brine and something else, something ancient and unsettling. It prickled at the back of my throat, a taste of forgotten magic.

Ahead, a colossal archway yawned, framed by two enormous coral formations that resembled the skeletal remains of leviathans. Within, a faint, ethereal glow pulsed, beckoning us forward. This was the entrance to the Oracle's chamber, the heart of Medusa's Lair, the place where destiny itself was said to be woven. Fear, cold and sharp, pierced through me, but the quest propelled me forward. Atlantis's fate, the hope of a golden age, rested on the knowledge we sought within.

We entered the chamber. The glow intensified, emanating from a crystalline pool at the center. The water within shimmered, its surface undisturbed by even the slightest ripple. Above the pool, suspended in mid-air, floated a woman. Her eyes were closed, her long silver hair drifting around her as if underwater. This was the Oracle, her form radiating an aura of both immense power and profound sorrow.

As we approached, her eyes flickered open. They were the color of the deep ocean, vast and unknowable. Her gaze settled on me, and a shiver ran down my spine. She spoke, her voice a melodious whisper that echoed through the cavern. Her words were not of greeting, but of warning.

The Serpent God, she revealed, a being of immense power banished long ago by Poseidon himself, had cursed Atlantis. This was no ordinary curse, but a venomous blight upon the very heart of the city, woven into its foundations, poisoning its future. The curse, the Oracle explained, was tied to the Serpent's Eye, a gem of immense power hidden somewhere within the ruins of the city. As long as the Eye remained, so too would the curse fester, preventing the prophesied golden age from ever taking root.

Her vision unfolded before us, a chilling tapestry of destruction. We saw Atlantis, not bathed in the golden light of a new dawn, but consumed by a creeping darkness, its magnificent structures crumbling into dust, its people transformed into monstrous shadows of their former selves. The Serpent God, a colossal entity of scales and shadow, emerged from the depths, his triumphant roar echoing through the ruined city. The vision ended, leaving us breathless, the weight of Atlantis's fate pressing down on us like the ocean itself.

The Oracle's words offered a sliver of hope amidst the despair. The curse, though potent, could be broken. The Serpent's Eye must be found and destroyed, its malevolent power severed from Atlantis. Only then could the city truly rise again. This task, she warned, would be fraught with peril. The Serpent God's influence permeated the city, twisting its creatures and its very magic against us.

But the Oracle also spoke of a hidden power, a force of balance that resided within Atlantis, waiting to be awakened. This power, she explained, was connected to the Golden Trident, an artifact of immense power wielded by Poseidon himself. It was the key to not only breaking the curse but also unlocking Atlantis's true potential. Finding the Trident, however, would be a trial in itself, for it was guarded by creatures loyal to the Serpent God and hidden in a place known only to the sea itself.

Her voice faded, the echoes of her prophecy swirling around us. The Oracle closed her eyes, her form once again still and serene. The vision, the weight of the curse, the hope of the Trident, it all settled upon us, a heavy mantle of responsibility. We left the chamber, the iridescent glow of the pool fading behind us, replaced by the ominous darkness of the cavern.

The journey ahead was daunting, a path strewn with unknown dangers. Yet, the faint glimmer of hope, the promise of a golden age, spurred us onward. We had a purpose, a mission. We would find the Serpent's Eye, break the curse, and usher in a new dawn for Atlantis. Our journey had just begun. The fate of a city, and perhaps the world, rested upon our shoulders. The air in the cavern seemed to grow colder, as if the Serpent God himself was aware of our presence, his shadowy gaze fixed upon us. The quest was no longer just a prophecy, but a race against a creeping doom.

2.1 Medusa's Lair

Slithering through a labyrinth of coral formations, sharp and menacing as a kraken's teeth, they entered Medusa's Lair. The water, normally vibrant with life and luminescence, held a stagnant, eerie stillness here. Sunlight struggled to penetrate the dense canopy of kelp and sea anemones, casting long, distorted shadows that danced like phantoms in their peripheral vision. The air, thin and laced with a metallic tang, clung to their lungs, making each breath a conscious effort. A sense of foreboding settled upon them, heavy and oppressive, like the weight of the ocean above. They knew they were treading on hallowed, dangerous ground.

The lair itself was a breathtaking paradox, a terrifying spectacle of beauty and decay. Giant clamshells, their pearly surfaces now encrusted with barnacles and shimmering with bioluminescent algae, gaped open like the jaws of monstrous beasts. Columns of once-magnificent architecture, now crumbling and overgrown with seaweed, hinted at the lair's former grandeur. Schools of phosphorescent fish darted nervously through the ruins, their fleeting light only enhancing the gloom. At the heart of the lair, a massive statue of Medusa dominated the scene, her serpentine hair writhing in perpetual motion, although carved from stone. Her eyes, though vacant, seemed to follow their every move, a chilling reminder of her petrifying gaze.

They moved cautiously, their senses heightened, alert for any sign of danger. The silence was punctuated only by the rhythmic drip of water and the distant, mournful song of a lone whale. Their fingers brushed against the cold, slick surfaces of the coral, sending shivers down their spines. The deeper they ventured, the more oppressive the atmosphere became, a palpable sense of dread wrapping around them like a shroud. They could feel the ancient power that pulsed within this place, a potent mix of beauty, magic, and menace. It was a power that could both create and destroy, a power they had to respect if they hoped to survive.

Suddenly, a ripple disturbed the stillness of the water. A figure emerged from the shadows, its form shimmering and indistinct. It beckoned them forward with a graceful, ethereal gesture. As they approached, the figure solidified, revealing itself to be the Oracle, her eyes glowing with an otherworldly light. She was draped in flowing robes of sea-green silk, her silver hair cascading down her back like a waterfall. An aura of wisdom and serenity radiated from her, calming their frayed nerves.

The Oracle spoke, her voice soft yet resonant, echoing through the chamber. She warned them of a powerful curse, a serpent god's vengeance upon Atlantis, threatening to plunge the city back into the abyss before its golden age could truly begin. The curse, she explained, was woven into the very fabric of Atlantis, a malignant energy slowly poisoning the city from within. To break it, they would need to embark on a perilous quest, a journey that would test their courage, their loyalty, and their resolve.

She revealed the steps they must take, the trials they must face. First, they would have to secure the Trident of Poseidon, a weapon of immense power, locked away in the god's underwater chamber. Then, they would need to seek the alliance of the Merfolk, a race of underwater dwellers known for their wisdom and magic. Finally, they would have to confront the serpent god himself, a being of immense power and malice, and defeat him in a battle that would decide the fate of Atlantis.

The Oracle's words hung in the water, heavy with the weight of destiny. They knew the path ahead would be fraught with peril, but they also understood the importance of their mission. The fate of Atlantis, and perhaps the entire world, rested on their shoulders. With a renewed sense of purpose, they vowed to fulfill the prophecy, to break the serpent's curse, and usher in the golden age of Atlantis. Leaving the lair, they carried with them not only the Oracle's warning but also the hope of a brighter future. The journey ahead would be arduous, but the reward was worth the risk: a world reborn, a golden age begun. The weight of the ocean above them seemed less oppressive now, replaced by the weight of responsibility, the burden of hope. They stepped into the shimmering light, ready to face whatever lay ahead, determined to succeed.

2.2 The Oracle's Vision

The air within Medusa's Lair hung thick and heavy, saturated with the scent of brine and something ancient, something unsettling. Phosphorescent algae clung to the cavern walls, casting an eerie green glow that illuminated the writhing forms of Medusa's serpentine hair, each strand tipped with a bioluminescent flicker. At the heart of the lair, veiled in swirling mists, sat the Oracle. Her form was indistinct, a shimmering mirage within the gloom, but her voice, when she spoke, resonated with the weight of centuries. It echoed not through the cavern, but within their minds, a direct transmission of thought and image.

The vision began with a vibrant, bustling Atlantis. Sunlight streamed through crystal domes, illuminating streets paved with gold. Citizens, adorned in shimmering silks and intricate jewelry, filled the marketplaces, their laughter echoing through the grand plazas. Atlantean technology, far surpassing anything known in the surface world, hummed with quiet power. Magnificent airships soared through the skies, powered by harnessed energy from the very heart of the ocean. This was Atlantis at its zenith, a beacon of civilization, a testament to human ingenuity and harmonious coexistence with the ocean's depths.

Then, the vision shifted. A shadow, vast and serpentine, slithered across the idyllic scene. It coiled around the city, its scales the color of a brewing storm. Where its shadow fell, the vibrant colors of Atlantis began to fade, replaced by a sickly, grayish hue. The joyous laughter turned to screams, the bustling marketplaces deserted. Buildings crumbled, their foundations weakened by an unseen force. The air crackled with a malevolent energy, a tangible manifestation of the serpent's curse. The very water surrounding the city seemed to turn against its inhabitants, whipping into furious whirlpools and dragging unsuspecting citizens into the depths.

The serpent itself remained largely unseen, a lurking presence felt more than witnessed. Its influence, however, was undeniable. The curse manifested in various ways, subtly at first, then with increasing ferocity. Crops withered, livestock perished, and a strange malady gripped the populace, draining their strength and leaving them vulnerable. The once-proud Atlantean fleet, the envy of the known world, lay in ruins, its ships either capsized by unnatural storms or inexplicably rendered immobile. Fear and paranoia gripped the city, turning neighbor against neighbor. The harmonious society, once the pride of Atlantis, fractured under the weight of the serpent's insidious influence.

The Oracle's voice echoed in their minds, explaining the nature of the curse. "The Serpent God, banished long ago for his treachery, seeks revenge upon Atlantis and its people. His curse, a slow and agonizing decay, will eventually consume the city and all who dwell within. The Golden Age, so close at hand, will never come to pass unless the curse is broken." The image of a single, obsidian scale, etched with intricate, pulsing runes, filled their minds. "This scale," the Oracle's voice continued, "holds the key to breaking the curse. It is hidden deep within the Serpent's Lair, guarded by his most loyal servants. Retrieve the scale, and you may yet save Atlantis."

The vision ended abruptly, leaving them blinking in the dim green light of the lair. The weight of the prophecy settled heavily upon their shoulders. The task ahead was daunting, the stakes impossibly high. The vibrant, thriving Atlantis they had witnessed in the vision, the promise of a Golden Age, hung in the balance. The serpent's curse, a slow, insidious poison, threatened to extinguish the flame of Atlantean civilization before it could reach its full brilliance. Their quest was clear: find the obsidian scale, break the curse, and save Atlantis. They had glimpsed the potential of a golden age, a world of peace and prosperity. Now, armed with the Oracle's vision, they knew what they had to do. The fate of Atlantis, and perhaps the world, rested on their shoulders. The air crackled with anticipation, the silence broken only by the soft drip of water and the distant hiss of Medusa's serpentine guardians. The journey to find the obsidian scale had begun.

3 Chapter 3: The Golden Trident

The colossal form of the Kraken surged from the inky blackness, its tentacles writhing like monstrous serpents. Each sucker pulsed with an eerie luminescence, illuminating the cavernous underwater arena. The air, trapped within the magically sustained dome, crackled with the creature's raw power. Our small vessel, the 'Triton's Whisper', tossed violently in the turbulent water. We had been warned of this trial, the ultimate test of worthiness before one could even approach Poseidon's Chamber. Mara, our navigator, gripped the helm with white knuckles, her face a mask of grim determination as she expertly maneuvered the ship between the flailing limbs. Kaelen, the stoic warrior, stood at the bow, his hand resting on the hilt of his ancient sword, its blade shimmering in the ethereal glow. I, Elara, chronicler of this perilous expedition, clung to the mast, my heart pounding against my ribs like a trapped bird. We were not warriors, not heroes in the traditional sense, but scholars, driven by the whispers of a forgotten prophecy. Yet, here we were, facing a creature of myth, our fate hanging precariously in the balance.

The Kraken's eye, vast and intelligent, fixed on our ship. A low growl, felt more than heard, resonated through the water, vibrating the very bones in our bodies. Then, with terrifying speed, a tentacle lashed out, narrowly missing the Triton's Whisper. The force of the near-miss sent a wave crashing over the deck, soaking us to the bone. Mara shouted orders, her voice barely audible above the roar of the churning water. We had to prove ourselves, not through brute force, but through cunning and respect for the ancient creature. Kaelen, understanding her unspoken plan, retrieved a large, intricately carved conch shell from his pack. He raised it to his lips and blew a series of long, resonant notes, a melody passed down through generations, a song of peace to appease the Kraken.

The monstrous creature paused, its movements slowing as the notes echoed through the chamber. Its massive eye, now holding a hint of curiosity, remained fixed on Kaelen. He continued to play, weaving a tale of respect and reverence into the music. Slowly, the Kraken's aggressive posture softened. Its tentacles, still immense and powerful, ceased their violent thrashing. The water around us calmed, the turbulent waves subsiding into gentle ripples. The creature, seemingly appeased, sank back into the darkness from whence it came, its luminescent suckers fading into the abyss. A sense of relief washed over us, as profound as the ocean surrounding us. The trial was over. We had proven our worth.

The path to Poseidon's Chamber now lay open before us. The heavy stone doors, previously sealed tight, slowly began to grind open, revealing a passage bathed in a golden light. We cautiously navigated the Triton's Whisper through the opening, leaving the Kraken's arena behind. The golden light emanated from the chamber itself, a vast circular space at the heart of Atlantis. At its center, resting on a pedestal of sculpted coral, lay the Golden Trident, its prongs radiating an otherworldly power. The trident, symbol of Poseidon's dominion over the seas, pulsed with a gentle, rhythmic energy, a heartbeat in the silence of the deep.

As we approached, a dark shadow fell upon us. Ares, the God of War, materialized before us, his eyes burning with a malevolent fire. He had been waiting, lurking in the shadows, ready to claim the trident for himself. His presence filled the chamber with a palpable tension, the air crackling with his barely contained rage. "Foolish mortals," he boomed, his voice echoing through the chamber, "you dare to trespass in my domain?" He raised his hand, summoning a spectral warhammer, its head crackling with dark energy. We were trapped, caught between the God of War and the powerful artifact we were meant to retrieve. Escape seemed impossible. Our only hope lay in the power of the trident itself.

With a desperate lunge, Kaelen reached out and grasped the Golden Trident. As his fingers closed around the shaft, a surge of energy coursed through him, through all of us. The chamber vibrated with the raw power of the sea god's weapon. Ares roared in frustration and charged, his warhammer arcing down towards Kaelen. But with the trident in his grasp, Kaelen was no longer just a warrior, but a conduit for Poseidon's might. He raised the trident, deflecting the blow with a force that sent shockwaves through the chamber. The clash of divine power resonated through the very foundations of Atlantis. We knew we couldn't defeat Ares, not here, not now. Our only option was to flee, to escape with the trident and find a way to use its power to protect Atlantis. Mara, ever resourceful, had already plotted an escape route. Using a combination of Atlantean technology and her own navigational skills, she activated a hidden portal, a shimmering gateway that pulsed with unstable energy. With Ares momentarily stunned by the unexpected power of the trident, we plunged through the portal, leaving the God of War and the crumbling city of Atlantis behind. We had the trident, but our journey was far from over.

3.1 Trial of the Kraken

The cavern trembled, a low, guttural groan echoing through the water. Illuminated by bioluminescent algae clinging to the jagged rock formations, the vast space felt both ancient and alive. Bubbles streamed upwards from vents in the ocean floor, creating shimmering curtains that distorted the already surreal landscape. Ahead, a colossal form began to materialize out of the gloom – the Kraken. Its eyes, two orbs larger than any chariot wheel, burned with an eerie, intelligent light. Tentacles, thick as ship masts and covered in razor-sharp suckers, writhed and explored the darkness, searching. A wave of palpable dread washed over the small band of adventurers as they huddled behind a towering spire of coral, the Golden Trident, cool and heavy, clutched in Arion's hand.

He knew, from ancient lore passed down through generations, that facing the Kraken was no mere battle of strength. It was a trial of spirit, a test of worthiness. This monstrous guardian of Poseidon's Chamber wouldn't yield to brute force; it sought something deeper, a resonance of purpose in those who dared approach the sacred trident. Fear threatened to consume them, a cold, paralyzing grip tightening around their chests. Lyra, her face pale but resolute, reached out and squeezed Arion's arm. The silent gesture steadied him, reminding him of their purpose, of the fate of Atlantis resting upon their shoulders. This wasn't just about them; it was about an entire civilization waiting to be reborn.

Arion closed his eyes, taking a deep breath, the scent of brine and ancient magic filling his lungs. He focused on the energy of the trident, letting its power flow through him. Images flooded his mind: the crumbling statues of a once-great city, the hopeful faces of the Atlantean people, the oppressive darkness of Ares' reign. These images solidified his resolve, pushing back the fear. When he opened his eyes, a new light burned within them – the light of unwavering determination.

He stepped out from behind the coral, the trident held aloft. The Kraken turned its immense gaze upon him, its colossal form still shrouded in shadow. A low, rumbling sound emanated from the creature, a sound that resonated deep within their bones, a sound that spoke not of aggression, but of... curiosity? Arion felt a pull, a strange connection to this ancient being. He understood, with a sudden clarity, that the Kraken wasn't their enemy, but a gatekeeper, a guardian of a power far greater than itself.

The trial wouldn't be a fight, but a communion. Arion lowered the trident slightly, extending it towards the Kraken not as a weapon, but as an offering. He projected his thoughts, his hopes for Atlantis, his unwavering commitment to its revival. The Kraken watched, its immense eyes unblinking. A single tentacle, tipped with a bioluminescent sucker, slowly reached out and touched the trident. The cavern pulsed with light, the energy of the trident resonating with the ancient power of the Kraken.

For a timeless moment, they were connected, two beings bound by a shared purpose. Then, as slowly as it had approached, the Kraken retreated back into the darkness, its immense form disappearing into the gloom. The path to Poseidon's Chamber was clear. A sense of awe and profound respect filled Arion's heart. The Kraken had not been conquered, but understood. This creature, a symbol of fear and destruction to so many, had shown them that true power lies not in brute force, but in the purity of one's intentions. The trial had not been about strength, but about heart. And they had passed.

They swam forward, past the now quiescent space where the Kraken had been, into a vast chamber bathed in an ethereal glow. At the far end, upon a pedestal of carved coral, rested the Golden Trident, radiating an almost unbearable brilliance. They had earned their way to this sacred place, ready to claim the artifact and fulfill their destiny. The fate of Atlantis, and perhaps the world, rested upon their next move. The weight of responsibility settled heavily upon Arion's shoulders, but his resolve remained unshaken. He would not falter. He would not fail.

3.2 Poseidon's Chamber

Sunlight, filtered through the fathomless depths, painted ethereal patterns on the chamber's coral walls. Pearlescent shells, each larger than a man, lined the perimeter, radiating a soft, otherworldly luminescence. Here, in the heart of Atlantis, lay Poseidon's Chamber, a sanctuary of forgotten power and breathtaking beauty. The air, surprisingly breathable, hummed with an ancient energy, a palpable sense of the sea god's presence lingering within the sacred space. We moved with reverence, our footsteps muffled by the thick carpet of sea flora that covered the floor.

This chamber, untouched by time and the ravages of the ocean, pulsed with magic. Crystalline structures rose from the floor, their facets catching the light and scattering it in a dazzling display of rainbow hues. Schools of bio-luminescent fish darted among the coral branches, adding their own ethereal glow to the scene. In the center of the chamber, resting on a pedestal of sculpted coral, lay the object of our quest: the Golden Trident. It shimmered, radiating an aura of immense power, its prongs humming with a barely perceptible vibration. This wasn't just a weapon; it was a symbol of dominion, a conduit to the ocean's boundless might.

The trident's golden surface was etched with intricate symbols, depicting scenes of ancient battles and mythical creatures. These weren't mere decorations; they told a story, a history of Atlantis and the power wielded by its rightful ruler. I felt a sense of awe wash over me, a profound understanding of the responsibility that came with claiming such an artifact. This wasn't just about fulfilling the prophecy; it was about inheriting a legacy, a duty to protect not only Atlantis but the balance of the entire ocean. As I reached out to grasp the trident, the chamber responded. The crystalline structures pulsed brighter, the fish swirled in intricate patterns, and the air thrummed with increased intensity.

A low hum resonated through the chamber, building to a crescendo as the trident seemed to call out to me. The symbols on its surface glowed with an inner fire, illuminating the chamber with their brilliance. I hesitated for a moment, captivated by the raw power emanating from the artifact. This was a force capable of both creation and destruction, a power that demanded respect and understanding. Gripping the trident's shaft, I felt a surge of energy flow through me, connecting me to the very heart of the ocean. It was a rush of pure, untamed power, a feeling of absolute dominion over the waves. But it was also a burden, a responsibility that I now carried with me. The chamber pulsed once more, then fell silent. The light from the crystalline structures dimmed, returning to their soft glow. The fish resumed their tranquil dance among the coral. I stood there, the Golden Trident in my hand, feeling the weight of Atlantis's fate resting on my shoulders. We had claimed the artifact, fulfilled the first part of the prophecy. But the true test, the battle against Ares, still lay ahead. With the trident in hand, we were no longer just explorers; we were champions, guardians of a lost civilization, ready to fight for its rebirth. The chamber, now bathed in a soft, serene light, felt different. It had acknowledged me, accepted me as the wielder of its greatest treasure. The journey had just begun. The true challenge lay before us, beyond the sanctuary of Poseidon's Chamber, in the shadowed depths where Ares waited, hungry for war.

We turned to leave, the trident's golden glow illuminating our path. The chamber seemed to bid us farewell, its soft light a promise of hope in the darkness that awaited us. As we swam toward the exit, a shadow fell across the entrance. A hulking figure, clad in dark armor, blocked our way. Ares. His eyes burned with a malevolent fire, his gaze fixed on the trident in my hand. He had found us, and the battle for Atlantis was about to begin. His presence radiated a chilling aura, a palpable wave of malice that sent shivers down my spine. The tranquility of Poseidon's Chamber was shattered, replaced by the tension of impending conflict. There was no escape, no turning back. We were trapped in the heart of Atlantis, face to face with the god of war, the fate of a civilization hanging in the balance.

He spoke, his voice a low growl that resonated through the chamber. "You dare steal what is rightfully mine? The power of Atlantis belongs to me." His words hung in the air, heavy with threat and the promise of violence. He raised his hand, a dark energy coalescing around it, forming a weapon of pure shadow. The battle was upon us. We had retrieved the trident, but now, the true fight for Atlantis had begun, right here, in the very chamber where it was meant to be protected. The peaceful sanctuary had become a battleground, and we were about to face the wrath of a god. The fate of Atlantis rested on our shoulders, on our ability to wield the power we had just claimed, the power of the Golden Trident. I gripped the trident tighter, its power surging through me, preparing to face the darkness that threatened to consume us all.

3.3 Claiming the Artifact

The chamber resonated with an ethereal hum, the air thick with the weight of ages. Sunlight, filtered through the crystalline ceiling, illuminated swirling motes of dust, each a tiny fragment of Atlantean history. Before them, resting on a pedestal of polished seastone, lay the Trident. It pulsed with a soft, internal light, its golden prongs radiating power. Intricate carvings depicting scenes of ancient battles and mythical creatures adorned its shaft, whispering tales of valor and sacrifice. This was no mere weapon; it was a symbol of kingship, a conduit to the raw power of the ocean itself. The very air around it crackled with latent energy. A palpable sense of anticipation hung in the chamber, a moment poised between destiny and destruction.

Hesitantly, I extended a hand toward the artifact. My fingers trembled, not from fear, but from the sheer magnitude of the moment. To touch the Trident was to touch the very heart of Atlantis, to accept the mantle of responsibility that came with its power. It was a weight I wasn't sure I was ready to bear, yet I knew I had no choice. The fate of a civilization rested upon my actions.

As my fingertips brushed the cool metal, a surge of energy coursed through my body. Visions flooded my mind – glimpses of a glorious past, a thriving kingdom beneath the waves. I saw kings and queens, philosophers and warriors, artists and inventors, all united under the banner of Atlantis. The Trident thrummed in my hand, resonating with the echoes of these forgotten memories. It was as if the very spirit of Atlantis was flowing into me, imbuing me with its strength and wisdom. The weight of the artifact felt less like a burden and more like a connection, a link to the legacy of this ancient civilization.

The visions intensified, shifting to scenes of destruction and despair. Ares, the god of war, his eyes burning with malice, unleashed his fury upon the city. Tidal waves crashed against the walls, buildings crumbled, and the once vibrant streets were filled with chaos. The Trident pulsed faster, its light flickering as if mirroring the city's struggle. I understood then the true purpose of the artifact – it was not just a symbol of power, but a key to restoring Atlantis to its former glory.

Gripping the Trident firmly, I felt a surge of renewed determination. The visions faded, replaced by a sense of clarity and purpose. The weight of the past, the threat of the future, all coalesced into a single, unwavering resolve. I would not let Atlantis fall. I would wield the Trident, not as a weapon of conquest, but as a tool of restoration, a beacon of hope for a civilization on the brink of oblivion. The chamber seemed to brighten, the ethereal hum intensifying as if acknowledging my decision.

A low growl echoed through the chamber, snapping me back to the present. The ground trembled beneath my feet, and the air grew heavy with a malevolent presence. Shadows danced in the corners of the chamber, coalescing into a tangible form. Ares had arrived. His eyes, burning with fury, fixed on the Trident in my hand. He radiated power, a palpable aura of destruction that sent shivers down my spine. Yet, I did not falter. With the Trident in my grasp, I felt a strength I had never known, a courage born from the echoes of a thousand Atlantean heroes. I stood my ground, ready to face the god of war, ready to claim the future of Atlantis.

He advanced, his every step shaking the chamber, his voice a thunderous roar. "Fool! You dare to wield the power of Poseidon? That artifact is not yours to command!" He lunged, his hand outstretched, attempting to wrest the Trident from my grasp. But I was prepared. Gripping the Trident tighter, I channeled the energy flowing through it, feeling the power of the ocean surge through me. I parried his attack, the clash of divine power echoing through the chamber. The air crackled with energy, the very stones of the chamber seeming to vibrate with the intensity of the confrontation. This was not just a battle for an artifact; it was a battle for the soul of Atlantis. And I was ready to fight.

The fight was fierce, a dance of light and shadow, of divine power and mortal determination. Ares, fueled by rage, unleashed a barrage of attacks, each one threatening to shatter the chamber and crush me beneath his might. But with each blow, I held my ground, drawing strength from the Trident, from the memories of Atlantis, from the hope of a brighter future. The chamber pulsed around us, a swirling vortex of energy, mirroring the chaos of the battle. Yet, amidst the chaos, I felt a strange sense of calm, a certainty that I was exactly where I was meant to be. This was my destiny.

I focused my will, channeling the power of the ocean through the Trident. A wave of pure energy erupted from the artifact, slamming into Ares, throwing him back against the far wall. He staggered, his eyes wide with surprise, the fury in them momentarily replaced by a flicker of fear. I knew I had him. This was my chance. With a final surge of strength, I raised the Trident, pointing it towards the heart of the chamber, towards the heart of Atlantis. A beam of golden light shot forth, illuminating the chamber with an almost blinding brilliance. The light pulsed, resonated, then expanded, engulfing the entire city in its warm embrace. And in that moment, I knew that Atlantis was safe. The Golden Age had begun.

3.4 The Shadow of Ares

The echoing clang of the Trident against the seabed still rang in their ears as they fled through the shimmering, labyrinthine corridors of Poseidon's sanctuary. Behind them, the enraged roar of Ares, a guttural sound that vibrated through the very water itself, spurred them onward. They had the Trident, a weapon of immense power, but it offered little comfort with the God of War hot on their heels. Corals, once vibrant and teeming with life, now recoiled from the destructive aura emanating from their pursuer. The very stones of Atlantis seemed to tremble in fear. They knew they couldn't face him, not yet. Their only hope lay in escape.

Panic threatened to overwhelm them. The twisting tunnels, moments before awe-inspiring in their intricate beauty, now felt like a claustrophobic trap. Every shadow seemed to conceal the vengeful god, every turn a potential dead end. They relied on instinct and adrenaline, their lungs burning, the pressure increasing with every desperate kick of their fins. Anya, the team's navigator, clutched a glowing orb, a fragment of Atlantean technology they had discovered within Poseidon's Chamber. Its ethereal light illuminated their path, offering the slimmest of hopes in the suffocating darkness.

The orb pulsed erratically, mirroring their own frantic heartbeats. Up ahead, a faint glimmer of light offered a tantalizing promise of freedom. They pushed harder, their muscles screaming in protest. As they drew closer, the light resolved itself into an opening, a submerged grotto bathed in the otherworldly glow of bioluminescent algae. They burst through the opening, gasping for breath, the pressure easing slightly. The grotto opened into a network of underwater caves, a hidden escape route the Atlanteans must have used in times of peril. They could still hear Ares's enraged bellows echoing through the water, a chilling reminder of the danger that lurked behind them.

They pressed on, deeper into the caves, the orb casting flickering shadows on the cavern walls. The algae painted the rough stone surfaces in a kaleidoscope of colours, a stark contrast to the grim reality of their situation. They were lost, deep within the bowels of Atlantis, with the God of War hunting them. The weight of the Trident, now secured in a waterproof satchel, felt heavy on Anya's shoulders, a tangible reminder of the power they carried and the responsibility it entailed. This wasn't just about escaping; it was about safeguarding the future of Atlantis, a future that hung precariously in the balance.

As they navigated the treacherous caves, they encountered strange and wonderful creatures, remnants of Atlantis's glorious past. Glowing jellyfish pulsed with an otherworldly light, illuminating hidden passages. Schools of iridescent fish darted through the water, their scales shimmering like scattered jewels. These fleeting glimpses of beauty offered a moment of respite, a reminder of what they were fighting to protect. Even in the face of such imminent danger, the magic of Atlantis persisted, a testament to its enduring spirit.

The sound of Ares's pursuit grew fainter. Hope flickered anew, a fragile flame in the darkness. They had gained some distance, bought themselves precious time. But they knew they couldn't afford to relax. Ares wouldn't give up easily. He would scour every inch of Atlantis until he found them. Their escape was just the beginning. The true battle was yet to come. They had the Trident, a symbol of hope, a weapon of immense power. But wielding it against a god was a daunting prospect, a task they felt woefully unprepared for.

Emerging from the cave system into the open ocean, the vast expanse of the sea stretched before them, offering a sense of liberation, yet also a chilling reminder of their vulnerability. They were exposed, adrift in a world both wondrous and dangerous. They looked back towards the shimmering outline of Atlantis, now receding into the distance, its magnificent structures a testament to a civilization on the brink of rebirth. The shadow of Ares still hung over the city, a dark cloud threatening to consume its light. But they also saw the glimmer of hope, the promise of a golden age, a future they were determined to fight for. They had escaped the immediate danger, but their journey had just begun. The Trident was in their possession, a powerful tool, but it was up to them to learn how to wield it, to master its power, and to face the inevitable confrontation with the God of War. The fate of Atlantis rested on their shoulders, a heavy burden, but one they were prepared to bear. They would find allies, gather strength, and return to challenge Ares, to reclaim their stolen city and usher in a new dawn.

3.5 Escape from Atlantis

The echoing boom of the collapsing tunnel entrance filled the water behind them. Debris swirled in a cloudy vortex, momentarily obscuring their escape route. Ahead, a narrow fissure in the rock face, illuminated by the eerie bioluminescence of deep-sea flora, offered their only chance. Ares, a towering figure wreathed in shadow and rage, materialized from the dissipating dust cloud. His eyes burned with a cold fire, fixed on the Golden Trident clutched in Arion's hand. The water churned around him, a visible manifestation of his fury. He raised a hand, and the seabed itself seemed to tremble.

Arion urged the others forward, his voice strained but resolute. "Into the fissure! Now!" He knew the trident's power, immense as it was, could not hold Ares at bay forever. The war god's rage was a tangible force, warping the very fabric of the ocean floor. He felt a surge of energy as he channeled the trident's power, a protective shield shimmering around them as they plunged into the narrow opening.

The fissure was a claustrophobic labyrinth, its walls slick with algae and unknown organisms. Sharp rocks jutted out, threatening to tear at their flesh and snag their equipment. The pressure increased with every meter they descended, a constant reminder of the crushing weight of the ocean above. Behind them, the enraged roar of Ares echoed through the twisting passages, a terrifying promise of his relentless pursuit. They navigated the treacherous path, adrenaline pumping through their veins. The darkness was absolute, broken only by the faint, ethereal glow of the bioluminescent creatures clinging to the rocks.

They swam in silence, each focused on the task at hand. The close confines of the fissure amplified every sound – the rasp of their breathing, the rhythmic beat of their hearts, the distant rumble of Ares' pursuit. The weight of the Golden Trident in Arion's grip was both a comfort and a burden. He knew that it was their only hope of escape, but its power was a double-edged sword, drawing Ares' wrath like a magnet. The fissure seemed to stretch on forever, a suffocating maze with no end in sight.

Finally, after what felt like an eternity, they reached a wider chamber. A faint, bluish light filtered down from above, hinting at an exit. Hope surged through them, a welcome reprieve from the oppressive darkness and the constant threat of Ares. They pushed upwards, their bodies aching with exertion, towards the shimmering promise of freedom.

As they broke the surface, gasping for air, they found themselves in a hidden grotto, shielded from the open ocean by a thick curtain of kelp. The grotto opened onto a vast, unexplored region of the ocean floor, far from the crumbling ruins of Atlantis. They had escaped Ares' clutches, but the cost was heavy. Atlantis, the city they had sworn to protect, was now lost, swallowed by the sea. The sense of loss was profound, a heavy weight settling in their chests.

Arion looked back towards the direction they had come, the memory of the city's grandeur and the warmth of its people now replaced by the chilling image of its destruction. The glimmering Golden Trident in his hand felt strangely cold. It was a symbol of hope, a powerful artifact capable of ushering in a new golden age, yet the weight of responsibility it represented felt almost unbearable.

They had escaped with their lives and the artifact, but their mission was far from over. The prophecy still echoed in their minds, a promise of a new dawn. They knew that their journey had just begun, and the challenges ahead would be even greater. They had escaped Atlantis, but the fate of its legacy now rested solely on their shoulders. The vast ocean stretched before them, an unknown expanse filled with both peril and promise. They were adrift, refugees from a lost world, carrying the weight of a civilization's hopes and dreams. The escape was a bittersweet victory, a moment of respite before the next chapter of their perilous journey began.

4 Chapter 4: The Rise of Arion

The roar of the crowd was deafening. A cacophony of cheers and jeers, the stench of sweat and fear thick in the air. Arion stood in the center of the arena, the hot sand clinging to his bare feet. He wasn't Atlantean royalty, nor a famed general. He was a gladiator, born into slavery, raised on the harsh realities of the fighting pits. His muscles, corded and scarred, a testament to countless battles fought, countless victories won. Today's opponent, a hulking brute from the northern tribes, snarled across the blood-soaked sand, wielding a spiked mace that glinted menacingly in the afternoon sun. Arion's weapon of choice was a trident, its prongs honed to razor sharpness. It felt strangely familiar in his grasp, a comforting weight that belied its deadly potential. This wasn't just another fight for coin and survival. This was a fight for something more.

He remembered the hushed whispers among the slaves, tales of a sunken city, a golden age lost to time. Stories of a powerful trident, wielded by a god-king, capable of controlling the very seas. These whispers had sparked a flicker of hope within him, a yearning for something beyond the brutal confines of his existence. When news of the recovered trident, now in the hands of those who sought to restore Atlantis to its former glory, reached the gladiator pits, it ignited a fire within him. He vowed to become a part of this resurgence, to earn his freedom not just from the chains of slavery, but from the despair that had shackled his spirit for so long.

This fight was his chance to prove himself. He would dedicate his strength, his skill, his very life to the cause of Atlantis. The brute charged, his roar echoing across the arena. Arion braced himself, the trident held steady. He moved with a fluidity born of years spent honing his body into a living weapon. He parried the mace's initial strike, the force of the blow vibrating through his arms. The crowd held its breath, anticipating a brutal slugfest. But Arion had learned to fight with more than just brute strength.

He used the brute's momentum against him, leveraging his smaller size and greater agility. He danced around the lumbering attacks, the trident a blur of motion. He aimed for precision strikes, targeting weak points in the brute's armor, exploiting his clumsy footwork. With each successful parry, each landed blow, the cheers of the crowd grew louder, fueled by Arion's unexpected display of skill and determination. He was no longer just a gladiator; he was becoming a symbol of hope, a champion for the downtrodden. His movements flowed with a grace that transcended the brutality of the arena. It was as if the sea itself moved through him, guiding his strikes, lending him strength.

Finally, with a swift, decisive thrust, Arion's trident found its mark. The brute stumbled, a guttural cry escaping his lips. He fell to his knees, defeated. The crowd erupted, their cheers a deafening wave that washed over the arena. Arion stood over his fallen opponent, his chest heaving, the trident dripping with blood. But his gaze was not on the defeated brute. It was on the faces in the crowd, on the hope he saw reflected in their eyes.

In that moment, he knew he was more than a gladiator. He was Arion, champion of the oppressed, a beacon of hope for a city yearning for its rebirth. Word of Arion's victory spread like wildfire through the streets of Atlantis. His display of skill and courage resonated deeply with the populace, many of whom were themselves struggling under the weight of hardship and oppression. They saw in him a reflection of their own desire for freedom, for a better future.

His name became synonymous with resilience, with the unyielding spirit of the Atlantean people. He became a rallying point, a figurehead for the growing movement to reclaim their lost heritage. He embraced the title of Champion of the Seas, not as a boast, but as a promise. A promise to protect the vulnerable, to fight for the future of Atlantis, to usher in a new era of prosperity and peace. He began to train others, sharing his knowledge of combat, instilling in them the same discipline and determination that had brought him victory in the arena. He organized the disparate groups of Atlanteans into a cohesive force, ready to defend their city, to stand against any threat, including the shadow of the war god Ares. He knew a greater battle loomed, one that would determine the fate of Atlantis. And he would be ready.

4.1 The Gladiator's Oath

The salt-laced air whipped through the arena, carrying the roars of the crowd. Arion stood in the center of the sand, his bare chest glistening with sweat, the trident heavy in his grip. He wasn't Atlantean royalty, nor a powerful mage. He was just Arion, a man forged in the fires of the arena, known for his brutal efficiency with the net and trident, a spectacle for the masses. Yet, today, something felt different. This wasn't just another fight for survival, for coin, for the fleeting cheers of the bloodthirsty crowd. This was for something more.

Around the arena, the faces of his fellow Atlanteans blurred into a sea of anxious hope. They looked to him, this gladiator, as their champion. The weight of their expectation settled upon him, heavier than any armor he had ever worn. He had witnessed the fear in their eyes, the despair that crept into their voices as Ares's influence spread like a dark tide across Atlantis. He had seen the once vibrant city, the heart of a magnificent civilization, slowly succumb to the war god's oppressive reign. He had felt the sting of the whip, the burn of injustice, and the gnawing hunger of a people deprived of their freedom.

He raised his gaze to the royal dais, where Queen Thalassa sat, her face a mask of stoic determination. Beside her stood Triton, his regal presence radiating calm amidst the surrounding turmoil. They had entrusted him, a simple gladiator, with the fate of their city, with the Golden Trident, Poseidon's own weapon. It was a gamble, a desperate play in a game with impossible odds. But it was a gamble Arion was willing to take.

Taking a deep breath, Arion lowered the trident, its prongs sinking slightly into the sand. The hushed expectancy of the crowd pressed in on him, a tangible force. He closed his eyes, recalling the words whispered to him by Triton, the ancient oath passed down through generations of sea warriors. It spoke of courage, of sacrifice, of unwavering loyalty to Atlantis and its people. It spoke of a duty to protect the innocent, to uphold justice, and to fight for the restoration of their rightful glory.

He opened his eyes, the arena coming back into sharp focus. The crowd, the royal dais, even the threatening sky above seemed to fade away. All that remained was the oath, echoing in his heart, a burning ember in the darkness. He gripped the trident tighter, feeling its power surge through him, a connection to the very essence of the sea. He was no longer just Arion, the gladiator. He was Arion, the Champion of the Seas, the protector of Atlantis.

"I swear," he began, his voice resonating with newfound strength, cutting through the silence of the arena. "Upon the sacred waters of Poseidon, I pledge my life to the defense of Atlantis. I will wield the Golden Trident with honor and courage, against all who threaten our people and our freedom. I will not falter, I will not yield, until Ares and his tyranny are banished from our land, and the golden age of Atlantis is restored."

His words hung in the air, charged with the raw emotion of his conviction. The silence that followed was deafening, then, a single cheer erupted from the crowd, followed by another, and another, until the arena was filled with a deafening roar of approval. They chanted his name, their voices rising in a crescendo of hope and defiance. Arion stood firm, the trident held high, a beacon in the storm. He was ready to fulfill his oath, to face the trials ahead, to fight for the future of Atlantis. The gladiator had become a symbol, a rallying point for a desperate people yearning for freedom. And in that moment, Arion knew he would not let them down.

The ceremony continued with the Queen bestowing upon him a ceremonial circlet of woven seaweed and pearls, a symbol of the people's faith in him. He accepted it with a solemn nod, the weight of responsibility settling deep within his bones. The cheers of the crowd washed over him, a wave of energy that invigorated him, strengthening his resolve. This was not merely a fight for survival; it was a fight for the very soul of Atlantis. He knew the road ahead would be fraught with peril, but he also knew, with unwavering certainty, that he was ready to walk it. The gladiator's oath had been taken, and the champion of the seas had risen. The fate of Atlantis now rested upon his shoulders, and he would carry it with pride, with courage, and with the unwavering determination to fulfill his destiny. The time for games was over. The time for war had begun.

4.2 Champion of the Seas

The roar of the crowd was a physical force, a wave crashing against Arion as he stepped into the arena. Sand, still warm from the Atlantean sun, shifted beneath his bare feet. He gripped the rough hilt of his borrowed trident, the familiar weight grounding him amidst the cacophony. This wasn't the polished pearl-handled weapon of kings, not Poseidon's fabled weapon, but a simple, brutal tool of the arena, honed for killing. Across the blood-soaked sand, his opponent, a hulking brute named Kragg, snorted derisively, his scarred face contorted in a sneer. Kragg, a veteran of countless battles, favored a wickedly curved net and razor-sharp daggers, a combination that had sent many a seasoned gladiator to a watery grave. Arion knew Kragg's reputation, the whispers of his savage efficiency. Yet, fear was a luxury Arion couldn't afford. He needed to win. Not for glory, not for the adoration of the crowd, but for something far more profound: the survival of his people. His childhood had been one of hardship, scavenging for scraps amidst the crumbling ruins of once-grand Atlantean architecture. He had witnessed the slow decay of his city, the creeping despair that settled in the hearts of his people under the oppressive rule of Ares. The war god had twisted their once-proud culture into a spectacle of violence and subjugation. The arena, once a place of honorable combat, had become a stage for his cruel amusement.

Arion closed his eyes, focusing his breath. He recalled the feel of the ocean currents against his skin, the rhythmic pulse of the waves, the whispers of the ancient sea deities that echoed in the deepest trenches. The ocean was his solace, his strength, the source of his unwavering resolve. He opened his eyes, a new calmness settling over him. He wasn't just fighting for himself. He was fighting for the memory of a glorious past and the hope of a brighter future. He was fighting for Atlantis.

Kragg charged, his net whistling through the air. Arion sidestepped with a speed that belied his size, the net snapping harmlessly past his shoulder. He lunged forward, the trident a blur of motion, its prongs aimed at Kragg's exposed flank. The brute roared in pain, the trident grazing his side. Arion pressed his advantage, a flurry of attacks forcing Kragg back, the crowd erupting in a frenzy of cheers and jeers. Kragg, though wounded, was far from defeated. He snarled, his eyes burning with rage, and with a sudden, desperate move, hurled one of his daggers. It spun end over end, a glint of deadly metal aimed directly at Arion's heart.

Time seemed to slow. Arion saw the dagger's trajectory, felt the rush of adrenaline, and with a swift, almost instinctive movement, deflected the projectile with the shaft of his trident. The dagger clattered harmlessly onto the sand. The crowd gasped, a ripple of awe spreading through the stands. Arion knew this was his moment. He spun, the trident now held aloft, and with a mighty roar, plunged it deep into Kragg's chest. The brute stumbled, his eyes wide with disbelief, before collapsing in a heap, the life draining from his massive frame.

Silence descended upon the arena, broken only by Arion's ragged breathing. He stood over his fallen opponent, the trident dripping with seawater tinged with Kragg's blood. The crowd erupted once more, this time in a unified roar of approval. They chanted his name, "Arion! Arion! Champion of the Seas!" The title resonated with Arion, a heavy mantle of responsibility settling upon his shoulders. It wasn't just a title earned in the arena. It was a calling, a destiny he couldn't ignore. He knew, in that moment, his life would never be the same. He was no longer just a gladiator, a survivor. He was a symbol of hope, a beacon in the darkness, a champion for a city desperate for salvation. He was the Champion of the Seas, and he would lead his people to a new dawn. He would reclaim the Golden Age of Atlantis.

5 Chapter 5: The Siren's Song

The rhythmic pulse of the ocean, a constant companion throughout their journey, now throbbed with a new, unsettling energy. A haunting melody, ethereal and seductive, drifted through the water, wrapping around them like silken threads. It was the Siren's Song, legendary for its captivating power, luring sailors to their doom on the jagged reefs surrounding Atlantis. Arion, gripping the Golden Trident, felt its power resonate within him, a counterpoint to the insidious melody. He recognized the danger instantly, a chilling premonition of the enchantment's grasp tightening around his companions. The song promised wonders, whispered of forgotten treasures and eternal bliss, tempting them to abandon their quest and succumb to the alluring depths.

The Siren's Song weaved illusions, conjuring visions of their deepest desires. For some, it was the embrace of lost loved ones. For others, it was the glory of conquest or the quiet peace of a life untouched by hardship. Each crew member grappled with their own personalized temptation, their resolve faltering against the song's hypnotic power. Arion, his mind shielded by the Trident's influence, saw his companions' eyes glaze over, their movements becoming sluggish and their expressions vacant. He watched in horror as they began to drift towards the source of the music, the treacherous reefs looming ever closer. Desperate to save them, he channeled the Trident's energy, sending a powerful wave of counter-magic surging through the water. The wave burst forth, a radiant shockwave of pure energy that shattered the illusions and momentarily disrupted the Siren's Song.

The sudden break in the enchantment jolted the crew back to awareness. Confusion and disorientation warred on their faces as they looked around, the remnants of the Siren's illusions still clinging to the edges of their minds. Arion seized the opportunity, his voice ringing out clear and strong above the returning melody. He reminded them of their purpose, of the hope they carried for Atlantis, and of the dangers that awaited them if they succumbed to the Siren's allure. His words acted as an anchor, pulling them back from the brink of surrender. With renewed determination, they fought against the song's influence, their minds now shielded by Arion's intervention and their own strengthened resolve. They knew that the melody would continue to tempt them, but they were prepared. The Siren's Song was powerful, but their will was stronger.

Navigating through the now turbulent waters, they steered clear of the treacherous reefs, guided by Arion's unwavering focus and the Trident's protective aura. The song's intensity began to diminish as they moved further away from its source. As the last strains of the melody faded into the distance, they found themselves in a realm of breathtaking beauty, a hidden oasis untouched by the Siren's influence. Vibrant corals pulsed with life, forming intricate structures that reached towards the surface. Schools of luminous fish darted through the coral branches, their scales shimmering in the filtered sunlight. This was the Coral Kingdom, a secret realm hidden deep within the ocean's embrace.

Within this vibrant ecosystem, they encountered the Merfolk, a race of aquatic humanoids with sleek, scaled bodies and flowing, iridescent fins. Initially wary, the Merfolk observed the newcomers with cautious curiosity. Arion, sensing their apprehension, approached them with respect and humility, explaining their mission to restore Atlantis to its former glory. He spoke of the threat posed by Ares and of their desperate need for allies in the upcoming battle. The Merfolk, moved by his sincerity and the Trident's inherent authority, listened intently. They had long suffered under Ares's tyrannical rule, his influence polluting their waters and disrupting the delicate balance of their ecosystem. Seeing in Arion and his companions a chance for liberation, they agreed to join their cause.

The alliance with the Merfolk was a strategic victory, bolstering their forces with skilled warriors and providing invaluable knowledge of the underwater terrain. The Merfolk shared their intimate knowledge of the ocean currents, revealing hidden pathways and strategic vantage points that would prove crucial in the upcoming confrontation with Ares. They offered their guidance, their weaponry, and their unwavering loyalty to the cause of Atlantis's rebirth. With the Merfolk by their side, a path to victory began to emerge from the murky depths. Hope, once a flickering ember, now burned brightly, illuminating their way forward. The Siren's Song, though a perilous obstacle, had inadvertently led them to a powerful alliance, bringing them one step closer to fulfilling the prophecy and ushering in the golden age of Atlantis.

5.1 Lure of the Deep

The haunting melody drifted through the water, a symphony of ethereal voices weaving a tapestry of longing and desire. It tugged at the edges of their minds, a silken thread pulling them deeper into the sapphire abyss. The Siren's song, a legend whispered among sailors and seafarers, now wrapped around them, an invisible net tightening its grip. Around the ship, the water shimmered, an iridescent mirage that shifted and danced, hypnotic in its beauty. The reef they had been following faded into the distance, replaced by a hazy, dreamlike landscape. Coral formations morphed into fantastical shapes, resembling castles and cathedrals, their surfaces pulsating with an otherworldly light.

Compelled by the enchanting music, they felt an almost irresistible urge to abandon the ship, to swim towards the source of the captivating sound. Arion, clutching the Golden Trident, felt its power thrumming against his skin, a faint vibration that resonated with the Siren's song. He recognized the danger, the seductive whisper of the deep promising oblivion. He fought against the allure, his mind a battlefield where willpower clashed with the enchanting melody. The trident's power seemed to offer a measure of resistance, a grounding force against the Siren's magic.

He shook his head, trying to break free from the mesmerizing spell. He saw his companions, their eyes glazed over, their movements sluggish and dreamlike. They were succumbing to the Siren's enchantment, drawn toward the shimmering depths like moths to a flame. He knew that if he didn't act quickly, they would be lost forever, consumed by the ocean's embrace.

With a surge of effort, Arion plunged the trident into the deck of the ship. A shockwave rippled outwards, disrupting the hypnotic rhythm of the Siren's song. The shimmering mirage flickered and began to dissipate, the fantastical coral formations reverting to their natural forms. His companions gasped, their eyes clearing, the spell broken. They looked around in confusion, their memories of the Siren's song fragmented and hazy.

"What... what happened?" one of them stammered, his voice still thick with the remnants of the enchantment. Arion explained the danger they had faced, the Siren's song almost claiming them as its victims. He cautioned them to remain vigilant, for the deep held many secrets, both beautiful and deadly. They had escaped the Siren's call, but the experience served as a chilling reminder of the unseen forces they were up against.

The silence that followed was heavy, broken only by the gentle lapping of waves against the hull of the ship. They had narrowly avoided disaster, a testament to Arion's quick thinking and the power of the Golden Trident. But the encounter had left them shaken, a stark realization of the perilous journey that lay ahead. The ocean's depths were not to be trifled with, a realm of hidden dangers and seductive enchantments.

As they continued their journey, a sense of unease lingered in the air. The Siren's song, though silenced, had left an indelible mark on their minds. They understood now that the lure of the deep was a constant threat, a seductive whisper that could unravel even the strongest of wills. They had to remain steadfast in their purpose, their focus fixed on their ultimate goal: the liberation of Atlantis and the dawn of its golden age.

But the experience also sparked a flicker of curiosity. What other wonders, what other terrors, lay hidden beneath the waves? The Coral Kingdom, a whispered legend among the merfolk, was said to be a place of unparalleled beauty and ancient wisdom. It was a place of refuge, a sanctuary from the surface world and its conflicts. Perhaps, Arion thought, an alliance with the merfolk could turn the tide of the coming war.

He shared his thoughts with his companions, his words met with a mixture of apprehension and hope. The merfolk were an enigma, their ways shrouded in mystery. But if they could secure their allegiance, they would gain a powerful ally in their fight against Ares.

The decision was made. They would seek out the Coral Kingdom, navigating the treacherous currents and hidden dangers of the deep. The Siren's song, a haunting reminder of the ocean's seductive power, had unintentionally led them towards a new path, a potential alliance that could change the course of their destiny. They sailed onward, their hearts filled with a mixture of trepidation and determination, ready to face whatever challenges the deep might hold. The lure of the unknown beckoned them forward, promising both peril and the potential for a powerful alliance that could reshape the fate of Atlantis.

5.2   Breaking the Enchantment

The Siren's song, a symphony of ethereal beauty, wrapped around them, pulling them deeper into the sapphire abyss. Each note resonated with a primal longing, a forgotten memory of a home they had never known. Images flickered in their minds: sun-drenched coral gardens, shimmering pearls, and faces of impossible loveliness. The lure was almost irresistible, promising an end to their struggles, a blissful oblivion in the watery embrace. The world above, with its battles and burdens, seemed distant and unimportant. Only the song remained, a beacon guiding them towards an unknown paradise. The rhythmic pulse of the music throbbed in their veins, a hypnotic drumbeat leading them towards their destiny, whatever it may be.

Their limbs grew heavy, their movements sluggish. The golden trident, clutched in Arion's hand, felt like lead. His grip loosened, the polished surface slipping against his palm. He fought against the seductive melody, the call to surrender. The faces of his companions, their eyes glazed over with a dreamy contentment, filled him with a desperate urgency. He knew, with terrifying clarity, that if they succumbed to the song, they would be lost forever. They would become empty shells, drifting through the ocean depths, forever enthralled by the Sirens' deadly music.

Remembering the Oracle's cryptic warning, Arion focused his mind, searching for a way to break the enchantment. She had spoken of a countermelody, a song of defiance that could shatter the Sirens' hold. He closed his eyes, concentrating on the memory of the Oracle's voice, the strange, resonant tones that seemed to vibrate with ancient power. He began to hum, a low, guttural sound that felt alien and yet familiar. The hum grew louder, resonating within his chest, pushing back against the Sirens' seductive call. As the sound intensified, a ripple of energy emanated from Arion, spreading outwards towards his companions. The glassy look in their eyes flickered, replaced by a flicker of recognition. They blinked, shaking their heads as if awakening from a deep sleep. The Siren's song, though still alluring, began to lose its power. The hypnotic hold lessened, replaced by a growing sense of unease. They saw the danger they had almost succumbed to, the abyss that had nearly claimed them.

With renewed determination, Arion continued to chant, his voice rising in power and defiance. The other explorers, spurred by his example, joined in, their voices blending with his to create a chorus of resistance. The underwater world around them shimmered and distorted as the two melodies clashed. The Sirens' song, once a symphony of irresistible beauty, now wavered and cracked, its power broken by the force of their collective will.

Finally, with a resounding crash, the enchantment shattered. The Sirens' song faded, replaced by the natural sounds of the ocean: the gentle sway of kelp forests, the clicking of crustaceans, and the distant calls of whales. The illusion of paradise dissolved, revealing the cold, dark reality of the deep sea. They had been close to the edge, close to losing themselves completely. The experience left them shaken but also strengthened their resolve. They had faced the allure of the Sirens and emerged victorious.

Now, with clear minds and strengthened spirits, they continued their descent, the faint luminescence of the Coral Kingdom beckoning them towards their next challenge. They had broken free from the enchantment, but their journey was far from over. The dangers of the deep still lurked, and the shadow of Ares still loomed large. Yet, they pressed onward, armed with the Golden Trident and the knowledge that they had overcome a formidable foe. The hope of Atlantis's golden age, once a distant dream, now felt within their grasp. They had faced the music and found their own voice, a voice of defiance and hope that would guide them towards their destiny. The path ahead was still fraught with peril, but they were ready to face whatever challenges lay ahead, united in their purpose and determined to succeed. The Siren's song had tested their strength and their will, and they had emerged stronger than ever before. They were ready to fight for Atlantis, ready to usher in a new dawn.

5.3   The Coral Kingdom

Shimmering, iridescent structures rose from the ocean floor, pulsating with an ethereal light. This wasn't simply coral, but a living city, sculpted by generations of merfolk. Delicate, fan-like corals formed ornate archways, while brain corals, massive and intricate, served as homes. Schools of vibrant fish darted in and out of the coral architecture, their scales catching the filtered sunlight that penetrated the depths. The water itself seemed to hum with a gentle energy, a testament to the magic that permeated the Coral Kingdom. Everywhere, merfolk, their tails shimmering with scales of emerald, sapphire, and pearl, moved gracefully through the city. Their long, flowing hair swayed with the currents, and their voices, melodic and haunting, filled the water with an otherworldly music.

This was a place of vibrant life, a hidden sanctuary teeming with activity. Merfolk artisans crafted intricate jewelry from pearls and shells, while others tended to glowing, bioluminescent gardens. The Coral Kingdom was not just a city; it was a living organism, a testament to the symbiotic relationship between the merfolk and their environment. They understood the delicate balance of the ocean and lived in harmony with it, protecting its resources and respecting its power. The very coral seemed to respond to their presence, growing and shifting to accommodate their needs. Here, the merfolk had created a utopia, hidden from the surface world and its conflicts.

The air, or rather, the water, felt charged with a potent magic. It emanated from the heart of the city, a massive, pulsating coral formation that glowed with an inner light. This was the Heart of the Reef, the source of the merfolk's power and the nexus of their magic. It was a place of ancient wisdom and profound energy, where the merfolk communed with the ocean and drew upon its strength. The Heart of the Reef pulsed with a slow, rhythmic beat, like the ocean's tide, its luminescence casting dancing shadows on the surrounding coral structures. It was a mesmerizing sight, a spectacle of nature and magic intertwined.

Approaching the city's central chamber, a grand hall carved from a single, enormous pearl, the heroes felt a sense of awe. The pearl's inner surface shimmered with a soft, iridescent glow, illuminating the space with a warm, ethereal light. Inside, the Merfolk Queen, adorned in a crown of woven coral and pearls, sat upon a throne of sculpted sea glass. Her eyes, the color of the deep ocean, held a wisdom that spoke of centuries spent beneath the waves. She greeted the heroes with a regal nod, her voice echoing through the chamber.

The Queen listened intently as the heroes recounted their journey, the perils they faced, and their quest to defeat Ares and restore Atlantis's golden age. When they spoke of the war god's tyranny and the threat he posed to the ocean, her expression hardened. The merfolk, she explained, had long sensed the growing darkness in the world above. Ares's lust for power was disrupting the delicate balance of the ocean, poisoning its waters and threatening the delicate ecosystems that thrived beneath the waves.

She extended a hand towards the Heart of the Reef, a gesture of offering and alliance. The merfolk, she declared, would join the fight against Ares. They would provide their knowledge of the ocean's currents, their mastery of underwater combat, and the power of their magic. Together, they would stand against the war god and defend the ocean's sanctity. The Queen pledged not only warriors but also healers, skilled in the art of using the ocean's resources to mend wounds and restore strength. Their knowledge of the ocean's flora and fauna, combined with their magical abilities, made them invaluable allies.

The alliance forged within the pearly chamber was more than a strategic partnership. It was a union of two cultures, both deeply connected to the ocean, both dedicated to its preservation. The heroes, representing the surface world, and the merfolk, guardians of the deep, found common ground in their shared love for the sea and their determination to protect it from the encroaching darkness. As they prepared to leave the Coral Kingdom, the heroes felt a renewed sense of hope. With the merfolk at their side, they knew they had a chance to defeat Ares and usher in a new era of peace and prosperity for Atlantis and the entire ocean. The Queen's final words resonated with them: "The ocean's fate is our shared destiny. Together, we will prevail." The words echoed the rhythmic pulse of the Heart of the Reef, a promise of resilience, unity, and the enduring power of the sea.

5.4   Alliance with the Merfolk

The shimmering, translucent walls of the Coral Kingdom pulsed with a soft, bioluminescent light. Schools of vibrant fish darted through the intricate coral architecture, their scales catching the light like scattered jewels. We had finally broken the Siren's enchanting call, a feat accomplished only through Arion's unwavering resolve and knowledge of ancient Atlantean lore. He had countered the Siren's melody with a protective chant, a low hum that vibrated through the water, shielding us from their manipulative magic. Now, surrounded by the Merfolk, their inquisitive eyes regarding us with a mixture of caution and wonder, we prepared to make our case. Their leader, Queen Coralia, radiated an aura of calm authority. Her long, flowing hair, the color of seafoam, swayed gently in the currents as she observed us. We explained our mission—to restore Atlantis to its former glory and defeat the vengeful Ares—and the vital role the Merfolk could play. Their deep-sea knowledge, unmatched combat skills in the aquatic realm, and mastery of underwater currents would be invaluable. Initially, Queen Coralia remained impassive, her expression unreadable. Her silence stretched, heavy and expectant, filled only by the subtle clicking of crustaceans and the distant songs of whales. I felt a bead of sweat trickle down my temple, despite the cool water surrounding us. We had gambled everything on this alliance. Failure here meant facing Ares alone, a daunting, near-impossible prospect. Finally, after what felt like an eternity, she spoke. Her voice, clear as a mountain spring, resonated through the cavernous space. She spoke of the ancient pact between Atlantis and the Merfolk, a pact broken long ago by the surface dwellers' greed and disregard for the ocean's delicate balance. The Merfolk, she explained, had retreated into the depths, watching with heavy hearts as Atlantis descended into darkness. Her words held a weight of centuries of sorrow, a deep-seated distrust born from betrayal.

Arion stepped forward, his gaze steady and resolute. He acknowledged the past wrongs committed by Atlantis, expressing genuine remorse for the actions of his ancestors. He spoke of a new Atlantis, one built on respect for the ocean and the creatures that called it home. He pledged to uphold the ancient pact, promising a future where Merfolk and Atlanteans could coexist in harmony. His words, sincere and heartfelt, resonated with a powerful sincerity, a stark contrast to the hollow promises of the past.

A ripple of murmurs passed through the assembled Merfolk. Queen Coralia's gaze softened, a flicker of hope igniting in her deep-sea eyes. She extended a hand, her palm open in a gesture of peace. The alliance was forged. A collective sigh of relief escaped our lips. We had gained powerful allies, a turning point in our quest. The tide, it seemed, was finally beginning to turn in our favor. Hope, like a newly lit beacon, shone brightly in the depths of the Coral Kingdom.

The Queen then detailed the Merfolk's unique abilities, sharing strategic insights into Ares's underwater fortifications and vulnerabilities. They revealed hidden currents that could swiftly transport our forces, bypassing Ares's patrols. They described the pressure points within the ocean floor, capable of triggering underwater earthquakes, disrupting Ares's stronghold. This knowledge, gleaned from centuries of observing the ocean's rhythms, was a treasure trove of tactical advantages.

We spent the next few days within the Coral Kingdom, strategizing with the Merfolk commanders. We learned their combat techniques, practiced fighting alongside them in simulated battles, honing our combined strength into a cohesive force. The Merfolk warriors, swift and agile, moved through the water with unparalleled grace. Their trident-wielding vanguard, coupled with our Atlantean soldiers, formed a formidable army, ready to face the might of Ares.

As the time for the final battle drew near, a sense of anticipation, mingled with trepidation, filled the air. We knew the risks were immense, but the potential reward – a golden age for Atlantis and a restored balance between land and sea – was a prize worth fighting for. With the Merfolk by our side, we felt a surge of renewed confidence, a belief that together, we could overcome the darkness and usher in a new dawn. The alliance, forged in the heart of the Coral Kingdom, represented more than just a strategic advantage; it symbolized a shared hope for a brighter future. It was a testament to the power of understanding, forgiveness, and the enduring strength found in unity. The whispers of Triton, which had guided us to this point, now echoed with a renewed clarity, promising victory against the looming shadow of Ares.

5.5 A Path to Victory

The shimmering Coral Kingdom pulsed with life. Rainbow-hued fish darted through intricate coral formations, their scales catching the filtered sunlight. Kelp forests swayed gently in the currents, creating a mesmerizing underwater ballet. Here, in the heart of the ocean, the merfolk resided, their city a breathtaking tapestry of pearls and coral, illuminated by bioluminescent algae. This was the domain of Thalassa, the wise and benevolent Queen of the Merfolk, and it was here that Arion and his companions sought an alliance.

Thalassa, regal in her flowing seaweed robes and crown of pearls, greeted them with cautious curiosity. She listened intently as Arion, holding the Golden Trident aloft, recounted their perilous journey, the escape from Atlantis, and the looming threat of Ares. He spoke of the prophecy, the promise of a golden age, and the need for unity against a common enemy. The merfolk, traditionally isolationist, had long observed the turmoil brewing in the human world above. They understood the devastating power of Ares and the destruction he could unleash upon the ocean's delicate ecosystems.

The queen's initial hesitance gradually gave way to a sense of shared purpose. She recognized the sincerity in Arion's plea and the power radiating from the Trident. The ancient weapon, a symbol of Poseidon's authority, resonated with the merfolk's deep reverence for the sea. She saw in Arion a leader worthy of their trust, a champion who could unite both land and sea against the encroaching darkness. With a solemn nod, Thalassa pledged the support of her people.

The alliance brought with it not only the merfolk's formidable fighting force, skilled in underwater combat and wielding enchanted tridents, but also their intimate knowledge of the ocean's currents and hidden pathways. This knowledge proved invaluable. The merfolk revealed a secret network of underwater tunnels, a labyrinthine system that bypassed Ares' watchful eyes and led directly to the heart of Atlantis. This clandestine route would allow Arion and his companions to infiltrate the city undetected, catching Ares off guard and striking at the very core of his power.

Furthermore, the merfolk possessed an ancient magic, a song of the deep, capable of influencing the tides and calming the fiercest sea creatures. This magic would be crucial in neutralizing Ares' control over the Kraken, a monstrous beast he had enslaved and intended to unleash upon the world. With the Kraken pacified, Ares would lose a significant advantage in the impending battle, tilting the scales towards Arion's forces.

The alliance also brought forth an unexpected gift: a shimmering pearl, radiating an ethereal glow. This was the Pearl of Tranquility, a potent artifact capable of calming the raging storms Ares could summon. It possessed the power to still the tempestuous seas, creating a window of opportunity for Arion's forces to advance. With the storms subdued, their ships would navigate the treacherous waters with greater ease, minimizing casualties and maximizing their effectiveness.

As Arion accepted the pearl, a sense of hope swelled within him. The alliance with the merfolk was a turning point, a beacon of light in the encroaching darkness. It was a testament to the power of unity, a demonstration that even the most disparate of beings could find common ground in the face of a shared threat. The path to victory was becoming clearer, the tide slowly turning in their favor. With the merfolk by their side, armed with the Golden Trident, the knowledge of secret passages, the song of the deep, and the Pearl of Tranquility, Arion felt a surge of confidence. He knew that they were now ready to face Ares and reclaim Atlantis for the good of all. The stage was set for the final battle, a clash that would determine the fate of Atlantis and usher in either a golden age or an era of eternal darkness. The weight of the world rested upon his shoulders, but he was ready to bear it.

6 Chapter 6: The Final Battle

The first rays of dawn painted the sky in hues of rose and gold, reflecting on the churning sea where two massive armies faced each other. Arion stood at the prow of his flagship, the Trident of Poseidon gleaming in his hand. The air crackled with anticipation, the silence broken only by the creak of ships and the hushed whispers of warriors. Across the water, Ares' war galleys, adorned with snarling wolf's heads, formed a formidable line. Black banners bearing the god's symbol of crossed swords flapped ominously in the wind. The final battle for Atlantis had begun.

With a roar that echoed across the battlefield, Ares charged forward, his chariot pulled by fire-breathing steeds. Waves crashed against the hulls of the ships as the two forces collided. The clash of steel on steel rang out, a symphony of destruction. Arion, imbued with the power of the Trident, fought with the fury of a storm god. He deflected Ares' fiery attacks with the trident, each parry sending shockwaves through the water. Merfolk warriors, their scales shimmering in the sunlight, harried the flanks of Ares' ships, their spears tipped with venomous coral. From the shore, Atlantean archers rained down arrows, a constant barrage against the invaders.

The battle raged for hours, a maelstrom of divine power and human courage. The sea ran red with the blood of both sides. Arion, though weary, pressed on, driven by his oath to protect Atlantis. He saw his comrades fall, their bodies swallowed by the waves, yet he refused to yield. He knew that the fate of Atlantis rested on his shoulders, on the strength of his arm and the power of the Trident.

Finally, Arion and Ares met in a clash of titans. The god, his eyes burning with rage, swung his war axe, a blow that would have cleaved a mountain in two. Arion, with a surge of strength, met the blow with the Trident. The impact sent a shockwave that rocked the very foundations of the ocean floor. For a moment, the two figures were locked in a stalemate, the air shimmering with divine energy. Then, with a final, desperate push, Arion channeled the full power of the Trident. A beam of pure energy erupted from the artifact, striking Ares in the chest.

The god screamed, a sound of pure agony and disbelief, as the divine power coursed through him. His armor shattered, his form flickered, and then, with a final, earth-shattering roar, he dissolved into nothingness. The black clouds that had shrouded the battlefield dissipated, replaced by the warm rays of the sun. The sea calmed, its surface reflecting the golden light. A hush fell over the remaining combatants, the only sound the gentle lapping of waves against the hulls of the ships.

The victory was hard-won. Many had fallen, their sacrifices ensuring the freedom of Atlantis. Arion, his body battered and bruised, stood upon the wreckage of Ares' chariot, the Trident held aloft. The remaining Atlantean and Merfolk warriors cheered, their voices hoarse but filled with joy. The war was over. Ares was gone.

As the sun set, casting long shadows across the water, Arion returned to the shores of Atlantis. He was greeted as a hero, the savior of their city. The people rejoiced, their faces lit with hope for the future. The Golden Age of Atlantis, so long prophesied, was finally within their grasp. The battle was over, but the true work had just begun. The rebuilding of Atlantis, the forging of a new era of peace and prosperity, would be a challenge, but one that Arion and the people of Atlantis were ready to face. They had faced the darkness and emerged victorious. Now, they would build a brighter future, a testament to the courage and resilience of their people. The final battle had been won, and the dawn of a new age had finally arrived.

6.1 Clash of the Titans

The churning ocean roared its approval as Arion, astride a colossal hippocampus, surged towards the war-god Ares. Triton's conch horn blared, a deafening call to arms that echoed through the submerged city. Sunlight, fractured by the waves, danced on the golden trident clutched in Arion's grip, illuminating the grim determination etched upon his face. Behind him, a legion of merfolk, their scales shimmering like captured stars, formed a formidable vanguard, their spears poised to strike. Above, a squadron of griffins, their riders Atlantean warriors clad in shimmering armor, swooped and dived, harassing Ares' monstrous cyclopean troops. The battle had begun.

Ares, a towering figure wreathed in shadow and fire, stood upon a jagged outcrop of black coral. His laughter, a harsh, grating sound, boomed across the battlefield. He swung his massive war-hammer, sending shockwaves that rippled through the water, scattering the merfolk and throwing the griffins off course. Around him, the cyclopes, each one a mountain of muscle and rage, smashed their clubs against the seabed, creating tremors that threatened to tear the very foundations of Atlantis asunder.

The merfolk, however, were undeterred. With a fluidity born of generations spent navigating the ocean currents, they weaved through the chaotic battlefield. Their spears, tipped with enchanted coral, found gaps in the cyclopes' armor, drawing ichor that glowed with an eerie luminescence. Above, the griffins, regaining their composure, launched coordinated attacks, their razor-sharp talons tearing at the cyclopes' exposed flesh.

Arion urged his hippocampus forward, his eyes locked on Ares. The war-god, sensing his approach, unleashed a torrent of fire from his outstretched hand. The hippocampus reared, its iridescent mane flaring, and deftly dodged the blast. Arion, with practiced ease, hurled the golden trident. It spun through the water, a streak of pure gold, before striking Ares' breast-plate. The impact reverberated through the ocean, throwing the war-god off balance.

Enraged, Ares roared and lunged towards Arion. The two figures clashed, the shock of their encounter sending waves of energy radiating outwards. Arion, despite his smaller stature, fought with the ferocity of a cornered lion, his movements guided by the trident's inherent magic. He parried Ares' blows, the golden trident humming with power, and countered with swift, precise strikes.

The battle raged, a maelstrom of clashing steel and divine energy. The mer-folk and griffins continued their relentless assault, whittling away at Ares' forces. But the war-god was a formidable opponent, his rage fueled by centuries of conquest and bloodshed. He fought with the desperation of a cornered beast, his every blow carrying the weight of his dwindling power.

As the tide of battle began to turn against him, Ares unleashed a final, desperate attack. He summoned a colossal wave, a towering wall of water that threatened to engulf the entire battlefield. The merfolk scattered, seeking refuge in the crevices and caves that dotted the city. The griffins soared upwards, barely escaping the wave's crushing embrace.

Arion, however, stood firm. He raised the golden trident, channeling the combined power of the ocean and Atlantis into the artifact. The trident glowed with an almost blinding light, pushing back the encroaching wave. Then, with a final, earth-shattering cry, he unleashed the trident's full power. A beam of pure energy erupted from the weapon, striking Ares squarely in the chest.

The war-god screamed, a sound of pure anguish, as the energy tore through him. His form flickered, his shadowy essence dissipating into the surrounding water. The wave he had summoned collapsed, harmlessly washing over the battlefield. Silence descended, broken only by the gentle lapping of the waves.

Arion, exhausted but triumphant, lowered the golden trident. The merfolk and griffins returned, their faces a mixture of awe and relief. The battle was won. Atlantis was free. The golden age could finally begin.

6.2 The Fall of Ares

The clash resonated across the ocean floor, a symphony of steel and fury echoing through the crumbling ruins of once-magnificent Atlantean structures. Arion, wielding the Golden Trident, moved with the grace of a dolphin and the ferocity of a shark. The trident, imbued with the power of Poseidon, crackled with an ethereal energy, each thrust sending shockwaves rippling through the water. Ares, the God of War, roared his defiance, his eyes burning with an unholy light. His armor, once gleaming, was now scarred and battered, a testament to Arion's unwavering resolve. He swung his massive warhammer, a weapon forged in the heart of a dying star, sending torrents of scalding steam erupting from the seabed.

Around them, the battle raged. Merfolk warriors, their scales shimmering in the ethereal glow of bioluminescent flora, darted through the ruins, their spears finding gaps in the armor of Ares' monstrous sea-serpent cavalry. The gladiator legions, inspired by Arion's courage, fought with a renewed vigor, their swords clashing against the tridents of Ares' elite guard. The water churned with the violence of the conflict, a maelstrom of blood and shattered coral. Giant squid, roused from their slumber by the cacophony, lashed out with their tentacles, adding to the chaos.

Ares, sensing the tide turning against him, unleashed a wave of raw power. The very foundations of Atlantis trembled, cracks spiderwebbing across the remaining structures. He bellowed a challenge to Arion, his voice a thunderclap that reverberated through the water. Arion met his gaze, the determination in his eyes unwavering. He knew that the fate of Atlantis rested on his shoulders, on the strength of his arm, and the purity of his heart.

Arion parried a blow from the warhammer that would have shattered a lesser weapon, the force of the impact sending tremors through his arms. He ducked under a wild swing and thrust the Golden Trident towards Ares' exposed chest. The God of War roared in pain as the trident pierced his armor, drawing ichor that shimmered like liquid gold. The wound, though not fatal, weakened him, disrupting the flow of his divine power.

Seeing an opening, Arion pressed his attack. He moved with a fluidity that belied the power he wielded, weaving around Ares' furious blows, each strike of the trident finding its mark. He fought not with hatred, but with a grim determination to protect the innocent, to secure the future of Atlantis. The merfolk warriors, sensing their enemy's vulnerability, redoubled their efforts, their spears finding chinks in his armor, their songs weaving spells of confusion and disorientation.

Ares, weakened and enraged, made one final, desperate attack. He summoned all his remaining strength, channeling it into a devastating blast of energy. The water boiled around him, the force of the blast pushing back even the mighty kraken who had joined the fray. Arion braced himself, the Golden Trident held high, channeling the power of the ocean into a shimmering shield.

The blast struck him with the force of a collapsing star, the light blinding, the sound deafening. For a moment, all was silent. Then, slowly, the water began to clear. Ares stood, his form flickering, his armor shattered, his eyes filled with disbelief. Arion, battered but unbroken, still gripped the Golden Trident. The power of Poseidon flowed through him, stronger than ever before.

With a final, defiant roar, Ares lunged at Arion. But he was too slow, too weak. Arion sidestepped the attack and with a single, swift thrust, plunged the Golden Trident deep into Ares' chest. The God of War screamed, a sound of pure agony and frustration, as his form dissolved into a shimmering mist of golden ichor, his power dissipating into the ocean.

Silence descended upon the battlefield. The remaining sea serpents, their master gone, fled into the depths. The kraken, its task complete, sank back into its abyssal lair. The merfolk warriors and the gladiator legions looked on in awe and relief as Arion, exhausted but triumphant, lowered the Golden Trident. The fall of Ares had brought an end to his reign of terror. The battle was won. A new dawn was breaking over Atlantis.

7 Chapter 7: A New Dawn

The iridescent glow of the Golden Trident pulsed softly, a beacon in the newly restored throne room of Atlantis. Sunlight, refracted through the shimmering water above, danced across the mosaics depicting ancient prophecies and heroic deeds. Arion, now King Arion, stood before the assembled Atlanteans and Merfolk, his hand resting on the trident's pearl-encrusted shaft. He felt its power thrumming through him, a connection not just to the artifact, but to the very heart of Atlantis itself. The air vibrated with a tangible sense of hope, a shared breath held for centuries finally exhaled. The long night of Ares' reign was over.

The rebuilding began immediately. Guided by the wisdom of the elders and the ingenuity of the Merfolk, the Atlanteans worked tirelessly. Damaged structures were repaired with a blend of ancient techniques and new innovations gleaned from the Merfolk's understanding of coral architecture. Gardens, once choked with dark magic, bloomed anew with vibrant, bioluminescent flora. The city, once a symbol of oppression, became a testament to the resilience and collaborative spirit of its inhabitants. Even the Kraken, its rage appeased by the fall of Ares, returned to its ancestral slumber within the deepest trenches, its presence now a protective ward rather than a lurking threat.

Trade routes, long severed by fear and conflict, were reopened. Atlantean vessels, powered by harnessed tidal energy and guided by Merfolk navigators, sailed to distant lands, carrying not weapons of war, but offerings of peace and knowledge. The exchange of ideas and goods flourished, enriching both Atlantis and the surface world. Arion established a council of advisors, composed of Atlanteans, Merfolk, and representatives from the surface nations, fostering a culture of mutual respect and understanding. He insisted that decisions impacting the ocean's health be made collaboratively, recognizing the interconnectedness of all life. This cooperative approach led to the development of sustainable practices that ensured the ocean's bounty could be enjoyed for generations to come.

Education became a cornerstone of the new Atlantean society. Schools, previously reserved for the elite, opened their doors to all, offering instruction in everything from marine biology and engineering to philosophy and the arts. The Merfolk shared their ancient knowledge of the ocean's currents, the secrets of bioluminescence, and the language of the deep. Atlantean scholars, in turn, taught the Merfolk about surface world history, literature, and the principles of governance. This cross-cultural exchange fostered a renaissance of learning, sparking innovation and creativity in every field.

Generations passed, and the Golden Age of Atlantis flourished. The city became a hub of knowledge, art, and technological advancement. Its people lived in harmony with the ocean, understanding its rhythms and respecting its power. The prophecy of a world reborn had been fulfilled. Atlantis, once a whispered legend, became a shining example of what could be achieved through unity, resilience, and a commitment to the greater good.

Arion, though aged, remained a guiding presence, his wisdom sought by leaders from across the world. He had witnessed the devastating consequences of greed and unchecked ambition and dedicated his life to ensuring that such darkness never returned. He established a system of governance based on principles of justice, compassion, and environmental stewardship, a model that inspired other nations to embrace similar ideals. He knew that the true legacy of Atlantis was not in its gold or its technological marvels, but in the enduring peace it represented.

One evening, as the sun dipped below the horizon, casting long shadows across the ocean floor, Arion stood on the balcony of his palace, the Golden Trident at his side. He gazed out at the city, bathed in the warm glow of bioluminescent coral. He saw children playing in the plazas, scholars debating in the academies, and merchants unloading their wares in the bustling port. He smiled, knowing that the sacrifices made, the battles fought, and the lessons learned had led to this moment of profound peace.

He reached out and touched the trident, feeling the familiar thrum of its power. He knew his time as king was drawing to a close, but he felt no fear. The future of Atlantis was secure. Its people were strong, wise, and united. The Golden Age had truly begun, and its light would shine brightly for generations to come. The whispers of Triton, which had guided him on this long and arduous journey, now echoed softly in his heart, a promise of enduring peace and prosperity. He closed his eyes, content in the knowledge that he had fulfilled his purpose, and that the legacy of Atlantis would live on, a beacon of hope in a world reborn. The waves crashed gently against the city walls, a lullaby to a kingdom at peace, a testament to the enduring power of hope and the unwavering spirit of those who dared to dream of a new dawn.

7.1 Legacy of Atlantis

The echoes of the final battle faded. The once war-torn city of Atlantis, now bathed in the warm glow of a renewed sun, began to stir. Buildings, previously scarred and broken, shimmered with nascent energy, their intricate carvings seemingly alive with the magic of rebirth. The Golden Trident, pulsing with Poseidon's power, rested in Arion's hand, a symbol of hope and the dawn of a new era. He surveyed the scene, a profound sense of responsibility settling upon his shoulders. This wasn't just a victory; it was a genesis.

Atlantis, freed from Ares's tyrannical grip, was poised for an unprecedented golden age. The whispers of the prophecy, once doubted and feared, now resonated with the promise of a brighter future. The people, once cowed and oppressed, now walked with heads held high, their eyes alight with the hope of prosperity and peace. The merfolk, allies forged in the crucible of war, swam freely in the surrounding waters, their harmonious songs weaving through the city's newly vibrant marketplaces. The very air seemed to crackle with a revitalized energy, a palpable testament to the city's resurrection.

The rebuilding effort commenced with a fervor unseen in generations. Atlanteans, inspired by Arion's courage and the merfolk's unwavering support, worked tirelessly to restore their beloved city. The intricate network of canals, once choked with debris and neglect, flowed freely once more, carrying not only vital resources but also a renewed sense of community. Gardens, once barren and desolate, bloomed anew, their vibrant colors mirroring the city's newfound spirit. The reconstruction was more than just physical; it was a spiritual rejuvenation, a collective act of healing that bound the Atlanteans together in a shared purpose.

Arion, despite the weight of leadership upon him, moved among his people with humility and grace. He understood that true leadership wasn't about wielding power but empowering others. He established councils of wisdom, drawing upon the knowledge and experience of Atlanteans from all walks of life. He fostered collaboration, encouraging the sharing of ideas and innovation. He understood that the golden age wouldn't simply be bestowed upon them; it had to be built, brick by brick, with the collective will of a united people.

Trade routes, long dormant, were re-established with neighboring kingdoms. Atlantean ingenuity, once stifled by Ares's oppressive rule, flourished, giving rise to marvels of engineering and artistry. Ships laden with goods and brimming with cultural exchange sailed to distant shores, spreading the story of Atlantis's rebirth and its commitment to peace. The city became a beacon of hope, a testament to the resilience of the human spirit and the power of unity.

Education became a cornerstone of the new Atlantis. Schools and academies were established, dedicated to the pursuit of knowledge and the development of young minds. The wisdom of the ancients, preserved in scrolls and whispered through generations, was now openly shared, enriching the intellectual landscape of the city. Arion believed that true prosperity wasn't just about material wealth but the cultivation of wisdom and understanding.

The legacy of Atlantis wouldn't be defined solely by its magnificent architecture or its technological advancements. It would be defined by its commitment to justice, compassion, and the pursuit of a better world. Arion established a system of laws based on fairness and equality, ensuring that all citizens, regardless of their background or social standing, had a voice and were treated with dignity. He established sanctuaries for the sick and the needy, places of healing and refuge where compassion reigned supreme.

As the years passed, the golden age of Atlantis blossomed. The city, once a symbol of a lost civilization, became a shining example of what could be achieved through unity, wisdom, and a shared vision. Its influence spread far and wide, inspiring other nations to embrace peace and cooperation. The whispers of Triton, once warnings of a looming threat, now echoed with the promise of a world transformed. The legacy of Atlantis wasn't simply a chapter in history; it was a testament to the enduring power of hope and the boundless potential of the human spirit. It was a reminder that even from the depths of despair, a new dawn can arise. It was a beacon of light, shining brightly across the vast expanse of the sea and beyond, illuminating a path towards a brighter future for all. The golden age of Atlantis had truly begun, a testament to the indomitable spirit of its people and the enduring power of hope.

7.2   The Golden Age Begins

The echoes of the final battle faded. Sunlight, unfiltered by the shadow of Ares, streamed into the crystalline waters surrounding Atlantis. The once-shattered city, scarred by conflict, began to mend. Buildings rose anew, crafted from shimmering coral and luminous pearls, reflecting the radiant dawn of a new era. The air, once thick with the stench of war, now carried the sweet fragrance of blooming sea flora. Fish, vibrant and unafraid, darted through the restored archways and colonnades, their scales catching the light like scattered jewels. This was a rebirth, not just of a city, but of hope itself.

Arion, weary but triumphant, stood upon the highest spire of the newly re-built palace. The Golden Trident, pulsing with the life force of the ocean, rested in his grasp. He looked out at the bustling activity below, a scene of joyous reconstruction. Atlanteans, their faces alight with newfound hope, worked tirelessly alongside their merfolk allies. The harmony between the two races, once unimaginable, now formed the bedrock of this rejuvenated society. He had witnessed the depths of despair, the crushing weight of Ares' tyranny. Now, he saw the boundless potential of a people freed from oppression, united in a common purpose. It was a sight that filled him with a profound sense of peace. His oath, sworn in the darkest hour, had been fulfilled.

The merfolk, their iridescent tails flashing in the sunlight, brought forth gifts from the deepest trenches – luminescent corals, pearls the size of doves' eggs, and ancient artifacts imbued with the magic of the deep. They shared their knowledge of the ocean currents, teaching the Atlanteans how to harness their power for energy and transportation. This exchange of knowledge and resources solidified the bond between the two civilizations, creating a symbiotic relationship that would ensure the prosperity of both. The Coral Kingdom, once a hidden sanctuary, now opened its arms to Atlantis, offering its wisdom and bounty.

Trade routes, long dormant, sprang to life. Ships, adorned with banners of peace, sailed to distant lands, carrying tales of Atlantis's rebirth and forging alliances with other nations. The city, once isolated by fear and conflict, now became a hub of cultural exchange and economic prosperity. Its markets overflowed with exotic goods, its streets buzzed with the languages of a hundred different cultures. Atlantis, reborn from the ashes, was becoming the heart of a new world order.

A new council was formed, composed of Atlanteans and merfolk, representing the diverse voices of the united kingdom. They drafted laws based on fairness and equality, ensuring that the mistakes of the past would never be repeated. Education flourished, with academies dedicated to the arts, sciences, and magic. Young Atlanteans and merfolk studied side-by-side, learning from each other and forging friendships that transcended cultural boundaries. The focus shifted from conquest and domination to collaboration and innovation.

The prophecy, once a whisper on the wind, had become a tangible reality. The Golden Age of Atlantis had truly begun. It was an age of peace, prosperity, and understanding, a testament to the resilience of the human and merfolk spirit. The legacy of Ares' tyranny had been replaced by a legacy of hope, a beacon shining brightly in the vast expanse of the ocean. The world, scarred by conflict, looked to Atlantis as a symbol of what could be achieved through unity and cooperation. The city, once lost to the depths, had risen again, more vibrant and magnificent than ever before.

Arion, relinquishing his command to the newly formed council, found solace in the quiet gardens of the palace. He had traded the clang of steel for the gentle murmur of flowing water, the roar of battle for the soft melodies of the merfolk singers. He had found a different kind of strength, not in wielding the Trident, but in nurturing the fragile peace he had helped create. He walked among the blooming flora, their vibrant colors a stark contrast to the darkness he had known. He felt the warmth of the sun on his skin, a symbol of the new dawn that had broken over Atlantis. The weight of responsibility had lifted, replaced by a quiet sense of fulfillment.

As the sun dipped below the horizon, casting long shadows across the city, Arion knew that the journey was far from over. Challenges would undoubtedly arise, new threats would emerge. But the foundation had been laid, the seeds of hope had been sown. The Golden Age of Atlantis had just begun, and its future, bright and shimmering, stretched before them like the endless ocean itself. The whispers of Triton, once a guide through treacherous waters, now echoed with the promise of a future filled with peace and prosperity. And in the heart of the reborn city, a new legend had been forged, a testament to the courage, resilience, and unwavering hope of its people. The age of Ares was over. The age of Atlantis had begun.

7.3   A World Reborn

Sunlight, refracted through the newly calmed waters, danced on the mosaic floors of the once-sunken city. Dust, disturbed by the recent upheaval, motes of gold and lapis lazuli, swirled in the beams, creating an ethereal atmosphere. The echoes of battle had faded, replaced by the soft susurrus of the returning marine life. Anemones unfurled their delicate tentacles, exploring the newly serene environment. Schools of vibrant fish, once driven away by Ares's dark presence, darted through the towering kelp forests that now swayed gently in the currents. The city, once silent and shrouded in darkness, pulsed with a renewed energy, a vibrant testament to its resilience.

The citizens of Atlantis, emerging from their hiding places, blinking in the unaccustomed light, moved with a hesitant grace. They touched the coral walls, still gleaming with traces of the recent conflict, a tangible reminder of the struggle they had endured. Tears streamed down their faces, tears not of sorrow, but of pure, unadulterated joy. Their whispers, at first tentative, grew into a chorus of gratitude, their voices echoing through the grand plazas and echoing chambers. Arion, standing tall with the Golden Trident held aloft, its prongs glowing with a soft, warm light, watched his people with a quiet pride. He had fulfilled his oath, not only as a gladiator, but as a champion of their collective hope.

The Merfolk, their scales shimmering in the dappled light, swam in graceful spirals amongst the Atlanteans. Their harmonious songs, once mournful laments, now soared with the joyous melodies of celebration. They offered gifts of pearls and coral, symbols of the newfound alliance, tokens of a future woven together in mutual respect and understanding. Their presence was a constant reminder of the strength found in unity, a powerful symbol of the bridges built between two worlds. The Coral Kingdom, once hidden and secretive, opened its arms to Atlantis, sharing its knowledge and wisdom, contributing to the restoration of the city.

Reconstruction began almost immediately. Damaged buildings, scarred by Ares's destructive reign, were carefully repaired, each stone replaced with reverence and care. The Atlanteans, guided by the wisdom of their elders and the innovative spirit of their youth, incorporated the natural beauty of the ocean into their architecture. Coral became the foundation for new structures, shimmering walls that pulsed with the life of the sea. Kelp forests were woven into living canopies, providing shade and sustenance. The city was no longer just a testament to Atlantean ingenuity, but a harmonious blend of nature and artistry.

Arion, relinquishing the mantle of warrior, embraced his role as a leader. He established a council of elders, representing all facets of Atlantean society, ensuring that all voices were heard in the rebuilding process. He focused on fostering education, encouraging the rediscovery of ancient knowledge and the exploration of new technologies. He knew that true strength lay not only in military might but in the intellectual and spiritual growth of his people. His wisdom and compassion resonated through the city, inspiring a sense of shared purpose and unity.

Trade routes were reopened, connecting Atlantis with distant lands. Ships, adorned with banners of peace, sailed the open waters, carrying goods and knowledge, forging bonds of friendship and cooperation. Atlantis, once isolated and feared, became a hub of cultural exchange, a beacon of prosperity and progress. Its markets overflowed with exotic goods and its streets buzzed with the vibrant energy of diverse cultures, enriching the lives of all who called Atlantis home.

The prophecy of the Golden Age, once a distant whisper, became a tangible reality. The world, reborn from the ashes of conflict, found a new center of hope in the heart of the ocean. The legacy of Atlantis, secured by the courage of its people and the wisdom of its leaders, would endure for generations to come, a testament to the power of unity, resilience, and the enduring spirit of hope. And as the sun set on the renewed city, casting long shadows across the revitalized coral gardens, a new era began, an era of peace and prosperity, an era where the whispers of the past finally gave way to the joyous symphony of a world reborn. The cycle of destruction and rebirth was complete, and Atlantis, rising from the depths, shone brighter than ever before.

9 798348 397159